PERFECTLY IMPERFECT

JACQUIE BIGGAR

WAVEFRONT PUBLISHING

This is a work of fiction. Characters, names, places, and incidents are either the product of the author's imagination or are used fictitiously, and any resemblance to actual persons, living or dead, business establishments, locales, or events is entirely coincidental.

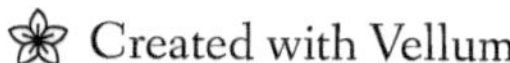

PRAISE FOR JACQUIE BIGGAR

Once every so often the world hears a new voice. Jacquie Biggar is the person to whom that voice belongs.

— Ben Reeding

I have read a couple of books from this author and I always get my mind blown when I read her work.

— Amazon Reviewer

Jacquie Biggar writes from the heart and hits you in the gut.

— Longtime Reader

For my extended Family, The Authors' Billboard
Without the friendship of these ladies, I don't know where I would be. They spur me on to be a better writer, support each other in times of distress, and cheer our successes.
Many thanks to Mimi Barbour for seeing something in me that I didn't know I had, and to everyone in the group for their love and kindness.
Jacquie

Love is always bestowed as a gift - freely, willingly and without expectation. We don't love to be loved; we love to love.

Leo Buscaglia

INTRODUCTION

What happens when Miss Perfection clashes with Mr. Casual? Chaos!

Georgina's in trouble. The startup money she borrowed from her parents' retirement fund is long gone and her dream of owning the next big thing in market-to-table cuisine disappeared with it.

Her only choice? Merge her company into the corporate giant, CLO, and hope she isn't making a huge mistake.

Rhys Turner is his father's progeny, born and raised to take over the empire when his dad deems him ready. Rhys doesn't mind the fast-paced lifestyle, though he detests the coldblooded mantra of the corporation- Buy from the weak and sell at a profit.

It's made his family millions. But now, just when CLO's reins are within reach, he's run into the one woman who could change everything.

1

Georgina

I hurry down the sidewalk, juggling three coffee cups. My umbrella insists on dancing with the cold north wind, doing little to keep me dry and a lot toward spilling the hot liquid all over my hand.

Mondays, ugh.

At least the rain cleared sidewalks from the normally bustling Seattle pedestrian traffic. Small mercies. Technically, it isn't my fault I'm late. My faithful twenty-year-old Honda decided today would be a good day not to start, and then I missed the transit bus that would have brought me straight downtown. I've ended up with an extra forty-five minutes tacked onto my morning commute, and the new CEO of *Bloomin' Right* is paying us a '*surprise*' visit this week.

I'd worked overtime all weekend to prepare. It made this morning's debacle even more frustrating.

Dodging a puddle, I reach for the tinted glass door at the same time as a male hand grasps the handle. Startled, I step back, banging into a solid chest. I swing around to apologize, and inadvertently catch my umbrella in the stranger's dark hair.

"Oh, no, I'm so sorry." I jerk the offending thing away from his head. The wind picks this moment to kick up and almost wrenches the blasted umbrella out of my grasp before I manage to wrangle it under control, the tray of coffees leaning precariously close to disaster.

Embarrassed, I glance at the rumpled man holding the door for me and attempt a friendly smile. "What are the chances two strangers would reach for a door handle at the same time like that?"

He stills from trying, unsuccessfully, to tame his rain-darkened hair and raises a brow. "I have to admit I've never been attacked by a deranged umbrella before," he agrees mildly.

He's tall, like really tall. I'm five-seven without my heels, and he towers over me. Even though the city is experiencing a cooler than normal spring, his skin is tanned a deep mocha brown, highlighting the most stunning blue eyes I've ever seen.

"You're staring," He takes the coffee tray out of my

lax fingers so I can close my stupid umbrella. "Bad luck to take an open umbrella inside."

I flush, cursing the tricky mechanism. "Thanks. I'm not usually so..."

"Klutzy?" he supplies.

I shoot him a glare. "Disorganized."

The cloth snaps closed, showering us with cold droplets of rain that stain my white dress pants. I stare at the dark splotches and sigh. "I knew I should have called in sick today."

Mr. Sarcasm take a swift step away and holds the coffee tray out from his body. "Are you?"

The dismayed look on his face *almost* cheers me up, except there is literally—I glance up at the looming gray sky—a dark cloud hanging over my head today, of all days.

"No, I just wish I was," I mutter, entering the foyer and holding out my hand for the coffee. "I can take those now, thank you. My new boss is coming to check up on our department this week and we've heard he's a real hard nose. I guess it has me more nervous than I thought." I press the elevator button and is relieved when the doors slide open almost immediately. "Well," I murmured, stepping inside and jamming a finger for the tenth floor. "It was nice to meet you. Thanks for your help." I gave him a winning smile and mentally urged the doors to close.

Ding.

The second set of elevator doors open, and a group of young, stylish-looking women step out laughing and chatting. Mr. Sarcasm glances their way and I let my eyes slide closed on a relieved sigh. No one else is getting on with me, so I'd have a minute to regain some equilibrium before reaching my floor.

The compartment lifts beneath my feet and I open my eyes—

"Claustrophobic, too?" Mr. Sarcasm says, leaning against the opposite wall, his head tipped to the side as though inspecting something strange.

"Shi... shoot. You scared me to death. It's rude to sneak up on people, you know." My heart is doing cartwheels in my chest.

"I wasn't *sneaking*, as you so eloquently put it. If you paid more attention to your surroundings, you'd probably avoid a few of the catastrophes you cause." He glances from my still damp slacks to his stained sneakers—which he teamed with what looks like an expensive navy-blue suit and powder blue dress shirt. Who wears running shoes with a getup like that?

Oh, no.

Oh, no.

Oh. No.

My stomach rolls with a sudden queasiness. I'd heard through the grapevine that our new CEO was a bit on the eccentric side, and I'd painted a picture of a grandfatherly man with a penchant for exotic pets. Something tells me I'm wrong.

So wrong.

I clear my throat. "Can I umm, press the button for your floor?" Since I'm practically guarding the control panel. *Please don't let it be...*

"The tenth—thanks," he says grudgingly.

Yep. I've just introduced myself to my new boss.

2

Rhys

This is lining up to be one of those days. The flight from Vancouver departed late, and the car service my PA hired got a flat tire on the freeway, leaving me stranded for forty minutes at the airport until another could be arranged. Serves me right for not grabbing a cab, but it doesn't help my mood whatsoever.

I'd argued with my father and the board of directors over the wisdom of adding to our investment portfolio at a time when the market is so unstable. Their answer; "We must strike while the iron is hot. These companies are selling for a tenth of what they're worth. If we don't step in and scoop them up, someone else will."

I'd heard that jargon, or something close to it, ever since I'd finished university with a master's in business administration, and been persuaded—none too gently—to repay the debt I owe my father by putting my education to work—for him.

I couldn't blame Dad, not really, but it annoys the hell out of me when my recommendations are ignored, leaving me to wonder why I'd spent the last eight years busting my ass to get a degree I can't even use.

My elevator companion is eyeballing my high tops with misgiving. I smirk, taking a selfish joy out of doing something my father would most certainly disapprove of—a style faux pas.

"Does your boss know you take time away from work to go on a coffee run?" I stare at her with disapproval. No wonder the company is failing if it's run so shoddily.

Her mouth drops open, then snaps shut as though she's biting back some creative language. She's cute in a librarian-meets-fashionista kind of way with an upswept bun thingy in her thick brown hair, oversized glasses that makes her green eyes huge, and wide-leg white pants hugging curvy hips. But she is still on my dismissal list.

If *Bloomin' Right* is going to have a second chance, it's my job to get rid of the deadwood—case in point, Miss Sassy Pants.

"My *boss*," she emphasizes, "Doesn't know his di...

plomacy from a hole in the wall." She lifts a brow as if to say, '*so there.*'

"Are you always so forthright?" I glance at the blinking numbers over our heads, five... six... seven... and try to slow my racing pulse. You'd think at thirty-six years old, I would have overcome my irrational fear of closed spaces, but, not so much. If I wasn't already running late, I could have taken the stairs. Instead, I'm counting on a pint-sized walking, talking danger zone to keep my mind off the fact we're in what basically amounts to a steel coffin.

"It's called honesty. You can't fire a person for that, can you?" With the umbrella hooked over her arm, wavy curls teasing flushed cheeks, and the tray of drinks in hand, she looks like a younger, sexier version of Mary Poppins.

My lips pull down at the corners. Great, now I feel like I'm here to get rid of the nanny. "Regardless," I intone, sounding way too much like my father for peace of mind. "You can't go around—"

The elevator jerks to a halt, causing a gasp of dismay from my companion as the coffee sloshes out of the air holes in little mocha-tinted bubbles, and a gusty sigh from me that we're about to be released from our prison. Except...

The doors don't open.

I look at Miss Sassy and she looks at me, and as one

we both look up in awed disbelief at the frozen number nine mocking our fears.

"Great. This is just great," Miss Sassy says. She backs into the opposite corner of the elevator and clunks her head a couple of times against the wall. "Did I mention I hate Mondays?"

I ignore her and jab my finger on the alarm button, working to stem my panic.

In. Out. In. Out.

Breathe.

"You need to call for help," Miss Helpful suggests, nodding toward the phone box on the wall.

Easy for her to say—literally. My throat is so tight I'm seeing black dots.

"Here, hold this," she mutters impatiently and shoves the coffee tray into my hands. She presses the call button, and after a blessedly short amount of time a male voice comes through the intercom.

"Stay calm," he says. "We've received your alarm and will have you out soon. How many are in the cabin, please?"

"Just two, Sam," Miss Sassy replies, glancing over my face with something like concern. "Hurry, will you?"

"Georgina, is that you?" The voice crackles with static.

She smiles and I frown again. So, she and this Sam are friends, are they?

"It is, I'm having a day." She laughs.

Laughs. I'm trying not to hyperventilate, and she's flirting with the handyman.

"Do you think you could save this for later," when she's unemployed, "and get us out of here, please?" My voice squeaks at the end, startling Miss Sassy —*Georgina.*

She shoots me a glare. "How long, Sam?"

"Well, these things take time. You just relax and we'll have you out of there as soon as we can. If you have any questions, feel free to call. And Georgina? Don't worry."

"Too late for that, I'm afraid. See you soon."

The sudden silence is more nerve-wracking than the tête-à-tête I've broken up. "Mind if I drink one of these?" I lift the coffee tray.

She shrugs. "Knock yourself out. They're probably cold by now, anyway."

With that endorsement ringing in my ears, I choose a cup and take a tentative sip. A bit more sugar than I normally use, and a shot of whiskey would have helped to steady my nerves, but beggars can't complain. Actually, after the early morning flight and the hiccups I'd encountered so far, it tastes damn good.

"Want one?" I offer her the tray.

"Gee, thanks." She rolls her eyes. "So, if we're stuck in here together, we may as well exchange names—I'm Georgina Michaels, and you?" She takes an appreciative swallow of the lukewarm brew and sighs. "This, I needed."

I set the last cup on the floor and lean against the wall, crossing my ankles and biting back a grin when her gaze seems to compulsively drop to my sneakers. I turn them so she can get a better look. "Nice, right? Limited edition Jordan's, light as air."

"Interesting choice with a business suit," she replies, eyeing me appraisingly.

"What is it you do, Georgina Michaels?" I glance at the floor numbers, then raised a brow. "We seem to be heading to the same floor."

Her gaze follows mine and her forehead furrows. "*Bloomin' Right*? Are you a new client, then?" She straightens and throws a hank of wet hair over her shoulder.

I almost feel sorry for her. She's probably a receptionist or secretary and needs the job, but I have something to prove to my father, so she's about to become a casualty of war.

"Something like that," I murmur, the coffee suddenly bitter on my tongue.

Georgina wipes a hand on her slacks, then holds it out for me to shake. "Mr.... I didn't catch your name?"

This is where things get interesting.

I take her hand, momentarily sidetracked by her soft skin. "I'm Rh—"

The elevator jerks, throwing us off-balance and Georgina into my arms. Shocked by the lush fullness of her breasts pressed against my chest, it takes a moment to realize something isn't quite right. I lean back and look down to see Georgina's wide eyes staring at the brown stain spreading over my favorite blue dress shirt.

"Oops," she says.

3

Georgina

I can't help it, giggles bubble out of my chest until tears blur my vision. The startled look on Mr. Sarcasm's too-handsome face is priceless. At least I'm not the only one having a less-than stellar morning. Most of it is my fault, but that's beside the point.

Then the warm pressure of his fingers on my waist registers and the laughter sputters out. Did I really just throw myself into a stranger's arms?

"Umm, sorry?" I peer up at him through wet lashes, intensely aware of his height and breadth and... manliness.

The fingers tighten briefly, sucking my hips into his like a peanut butter and jelly sandwich, before he lets me go and I stumble backward just as the elevator doors slide open.

"I'm so sorry. We worked on an electrical issue over the weekend and I thought... Georgina?" Sam sputters to a halt, gazing from me to the stranger with wary eyes. "Everything okay here?"

My cheeks burn. "Fine, Sam. Thanks for saving the day." I smile at the kindly caretaker and reach down for the leftover coffee. "It's probably cold, sorry."

Sam accepts the cup and takes an appreciative whiff. "You didn't need to, but I'm glad you did."

"I remember my debts. I'm going to owe you big time now." I chuckle and escape the faulty elevator. "Next time I'm taking the stairs. It's good cardio, anyway."

The weight of the stranger's gaze reminds me of my duties. I glance over my shoulder to invite him to follow and catch him staring at my butt. "What?" I ask, twisting and swiping at a spot I can't see.

"I was just thinking you don't need to take the stairs, that's all." He looks at me with denim-blue eyes and I feel myself falling into their bottomless depths.

"Well, if you don't need me anymore, I'd better get back to my desk." Sam raises a bushy gray brow with a few squiggly black hairs interspersed like random lightning bolts. "You sure you're all right now?" He straightens, throwing a growing paunch toward our new client.

I hurry to step between them and usher Sam the short distance to the second elevator. "I hope you have better luck than I did," I tease, tapping the down arrow. "Don't worry about him," I nod over my shoulder, "he's harmless." *I hope.*

The bell dings and the doors open to reveal Ella and Tom, my assistants, staring at each other with anger darkening their expressions.

What now?

Tom straightens first, and brushes by Sam and me with a muttered, "Women."

Ella shrugs half-heartedly. "Hi, boss."

I so don't have time for this. But Ella is my friend and it's obvious something is wrong.

I sigh and turn back to my potential client. "Could you give me five minutes? I need to... handle an important matter. Just go in and have a look around. I won't be long."

Mr. Blue Eyes—I really need to get his name—takes one glance at the miserable Ella and nods. "Of course. Take your time."

I watch him stride to the double frosted-glass doors with *Bloomin' Right* scrolled in Sattersoon Script and disappear inside. We can't afford to lose customers, so hopefully he'll wait.

Sam looks as though he want to be anywhere but standing with a sniffling woman. I can't blame him. It isn't my idea of a good time, either.

A sectional sofa is nestled into the far corner with a

couple of club chairs and a glass-topped table covered by an assortment of fashion and food magazines sprawled across the top. A large bay window gives an inspiring view of the Seattle Space Needle against the grim sky.

"Come on, Ella. Let's get out of Sam's way and you can tell me what has your knickers in a knot." Grandma Jenkins used to say that to us kids all the time. Fond memories tighten my throat. Six months and I still miss her every day.

"So," I hand over a box of tissues, "what did he do this time?"

"Tom is such a jerk," she mumbles behind the tissue. "What did I ever see in him?"

I grimace. Tom is a good friend. I hate dissing him behind his back. "Maybe it was a miscommunication?" I offer hopefully.

"He was communicating just fine—with that skank, Sue Evens." She flops back and stares up at the ceiling. "Why can't I meet someone who loves me for me?"

"Oh, honey, if Tom doesn't realize what an amazing, sweet, kind, sexy woman you are, it's his loss." I lean over to give her a hug, inhaling the jasmine shampoo she swears keeps her tight dark curls under control. Her chunky necklace cuts into my cheek, but I hold firm, determined to instill my words into her heart.

Why is it we women allow ourselves to be downtrodden by the opinions of others? Men never seem to have trouble ignoring things they don't want to hear. We could take a lesson from them.

By the time I sit back my shoulder is damp, but the wry smile on Ella's lips tell me the worst is over.

"Sexy, huh?"

I grin, relieved. "Absolutely. Let's go out Friday night and you can see for yourself. Wear that slinky red dress you've been saving for a special occasion and you'll have your choice of dance partners, just you wait and see."

"Are you seriously considering a night off? I must look even more pathetic than I thought." Ella dabs at the moisture lingering on long, curling lashes.

I glance at the company doors and rise, torn between cheering my friend up and saving our business.

"Go, I'm just whining," Ella says, rising as well. "You can get me drunk Friday and we'll commiserate together. By the way, who's the hunk?"

My cheeks grow warm. "I never noticed." I tap my nose to make sure it stays the same size. "He's a prospective client. I really need to get in there and wow him with our greatness."

Ella smiles and gives me a light push. “Go get ’im, Boss.”

“I don’t want him—or any man. I’ll be happy with a contract, thank you very much.” It sounds good, too bad I have a feeling my heart decided to go for a different endgame.

4

Rhys

The moment I step through *Bloomin' Right's* double doors I'm transported into another world. One colored in shades of grass green, pale yellow, and soft grays. The open floor plan allows staff members sitting on balance balls at modern desks to easily exchange ideas. I'm not sure what I expected, but this contemporary, seemingly profitable executive corporation isn't it.

"Can I help you?" A young woman pops up from behind the long receptionist's counter that separates me from the main part of the office space.

I give her my friendliest smile and wander over to look at a few of the pamphlets lined up like soldiers on the counter. "I have an appointment to meet with a Ms. Michaels? She should be expecting me—Rhys Turner with CLO Investments."

The welcoming expression on the other woman's face dies a sudden death and the office behind her goes silent. She turns and sends a slightly panicked glance at the preppy guy watching our exchange with interest.

"Is there a problem?" I get the feeling I'm about to get the classic runaround. Ms. Michaels might as well accept her fate. Trying to avoid me is only going to prolong the inevitable.

"No," the young woman chirps overloud. "She's looking forward to your meeting, she's been talking about it for weeks."

I bet.

"Let me see if she's available. Jeremy can answer any questions you may have while you wait." She gives preppy guy a verbal nudge and scurries to the back where frosted glass offices separate management from the front-end hub.

Jeremy rises and ambles over in a pink polo shirt, dark jeans and black sneakers with white soles. I like him already.

"What do you think of them?" he asks, nodding toward the colorful pamphlets littering the countertop.

I take another look at the one I've been mangling. The concept isn't new; food boxes for home delivery are a growing trend for busy millennials. *Bloomin' Right* took the idea a step further with organic products and unique recipes incorporating herbs and flowers known for their nutritional benefits. The reasons they're failing is bad marketing and high expenses—something I excel at. Too bad dear old Dad has already made the unilateral decision to sell.

"Your work?" I tap the pamphlet, suitably impressed.

"Georgina's concept, we just handled the details." He gives me a look as though I should know who this Georgina person is and maybe even bow at her brilliance.

I have news for him; if she's the head of marketing, she needs to go back to school. The colors are all wrong for consumer interest, the font is too small, and the descriptions are vague. On the upside, the photography is exceptional, as are the appetizing meals shown.

"Have you worked here long?" He looks as though he's fresh out of college, but hey, it could be the Princeton haircut giving that impression.

"Four years," he says, giving me an up and down appraisal. "Are you thinking of joining the team?"

"In a matter of speaking." I avoid the invitation glittering in his eyes to do another search for the missing Ms. Michaels. "I met your receptionist on my way up here. She's... different." That's a mild way of putting it, though I can't forget the feel of her lush body in my arms.

Jeremy raises his brow. "Receptionist? I think there's been a—"

"Tom will see you now." The young woman called, towing the disgruntled man from the elevator behind her.

He steps forward, his hand leading the way. "Tom Fairlane, executive assistant to Ms. Michaels. We're looking forward to presenting our company for your inspection."

Professional.

Polite.

Full of crap.

I'm not a fan of clammy hands or shifty eyes but can play the game with the best of them. I give his hand a stiff shake before stepping out of the radius of his cologne. I wouldn't be surprised if he has a scurry of squirrels following him on his walks through the park.

"I must admit I expected Ms. Michaels to meet me. Maybe she's not as invested in this enterprise as you think." Partly, I'm annoyed at the missing manager, but I also like to incorporate what I call the shock factor. If there's little company loyalty, it tells me more than a financial report about how the business has been run.

Jeremy sputters. "Georgina loves this corporation. She built it from the ground up. She's easily the hardest worker here." He glowers at me, all hints of his previous attraction to me gone.

The perky brunette agrees. "I haven't been on the job long, but Ms. Michaels is the best. She always has time for questions and even brings us coffee Monday mornings."

Coffee?

I absently rub the still damp stain on my shirt. Is it possible…?

"Is your boss—?"

"Right behind you, *Mr. Turner*. Sorry I'm late."

Shaking my head, I chuckle. "I should have known."

"Have you two met?" Brunette asks, her head tipped in confusion.

"In the elevator," Ms. Michaels—Georgina—explains as I turn to the disheveled woman and her friend, who looks as though she'd been put through the wringer. "Thanks for taking care of him until I could take over, Patty. Your coffee had a mishap," she glances at my chest and away. "I'll grab you one later, okay?"

"She's a staff member, Georgina. It's hardly necessary," Tom says, arms crossed as he stares at his girlfriend.

"Mind your own business, Tom," Ella snaps, her posture aggressive. "At least Georgina is honest. Unlike some people we know," she adds under her breath.

Georgina gives a nervous laugh and wrings her

hands. "Tom, I need the files I asked you to work on, please? My office in five minutes?"

Tom gives a stiff nod. "Yeah, sure. You're the boss." He spins on his heel and strides away, looking neither left nor right. A moment later a door slams, reverberating down the hall.

"I'm sorry, Mr. Turner, he's actually a nice guy. Not that you'd know it by today's exhibition." Ella gives a shaky smile and hurries toward the women's washroom set against the far wall.

"Well, schematics to create and all that," Jeremy murmurs, heading back to his desk.

Patty hesitated as though not sure where to go, then shrugs and follows Ella to the washroom.

Which leaves me with my new manager. This is turning into a Monday for the books.

5

Georgina

So far as first impressions go, I'm batting zero. I'm not sure how, but I need to change Mr. Turner's opinion of our professionalism fast or we're doomed. I only wish that was an exaggeration, but the truth is, without the CLO Corporation, *Bloomin' Right* is only months away from bankruptcy. I can't bear the thought of giving her to a corporate giant, but I can't face losing my baby either. Rock meet hard place.

"Well, Mr. Turner, if you'll follow me..." I give him what I hope is a friendly smile—minus bared teeth—and lead him to my inner sanctum. The office is modest in size, but I like to think it makes up for it in personality. The walls are a soothing dove gray, except for the one behind my desk, which is highlighted with a single wide brushstroke of magenta laid diagonally from top to bottom. The floors are engineered hardwood in a warm oak, as is my oversized desk. A giant potted fern —a gift from Ella—adds a pleasing touch and draws the eye to my list of credentials and awards, of which there are many, might I say, on the opposite wall.

I stand aside to let Mr. Turner take in the décor and am let down when he simply chooses one of the straight-back chairs and drops his admittedly fine derriere onto the seat.

I let out a slow sigh, beg the gods for patience, and close the door before rounding the desk to my own chair.

"So, Mr. Turner—"

"Rhys," he interrupts. "If we're going to be working together for the foreseeable future, I think we can dispense with formality, don't you?" He pats his coffee-stained shirt as though to remind me we've gone long past convention.

"Of course," I reluctantly agree. Reluctant because calling this man by his first name feels way too personal. "So, *Rhys*," I start again, "I can't tell you how grateful we are that CLO considers *Bloomin' Right* viable enough to go into partnership with us. I promise you won't regret the decision."

Rhys unfastens the single button holding his expensive wool suit jacket closed and crosses his leg at the knee. "I'm sure you'll understand if I hold off on the celebrations just yet. You and I both know your little venture here," he waves a hand encompassing the business, "is in serious financial trouble, or you wouldn't need CLO to bail you out.

"I suggest we start with your accounts and go from there. I want a full picture of the last six months sales to see how the company is trending. We can work on the rest later."

I stare at the hand holding his ankle as his foot in that silly sneaker tap-taps along with his chatter. It's a nice hand, long and narrow, with a complicated-looking watch covering his wrist. He doesn't have hairy knuckles like my ex, Kevin, either. I mentally add a checkmark in the pro column, though his attitude is all con.

"Of course. Tom should be—"

The door swings open after a preemptive knock and Tom strides in, a stack of folders under one arm.

"Don't you have bookkeeping software on your computer system?" Rhys asks, his brow furrowing.

"We keep hard copies as backup," Tom says. "Safer that way." He gives Rhys a duh look that doesn't go unnoticed by our guest.

"May I?" Rhys holds out his elegant fingers for the folders. Since when did I gain a fascination with a man's appendages anyway? Ringless appendages.

Tom glances at me, and I give a short nod. There

isn't anything in those papers that CLO isn't already aware of—I don't believe in keeping secrets from my benefactor.

Rather than taking a seat, Tom sets a shoulder against the wall and crosses his arms while Rhys skims over the information. I shoot him an annoyed glare, but it bounces off his arrogant chest—men.

The page turning slows and my heart speeds up in counterpoint. "Is there a problem?" I ask with bated breath.

Rhys glances between me and Tom, then reads from the paper. "Expenses for March 2018 convention. Fifty-five hundred in hotel fees, two thousand for car service, four thousand to convention costs, and twenty-eight hundred for meals." He shakes his head and whistles under his breath. "Talk about an executive budget on a pauper's pocketbook. What were you thinking?"

Tom stiffens. "Conventions are a key source of advertising. If you don't go into it with both feet, why would anyone buy into your pitch?"

Privately, I agree with Tom, but follow the first rule of commerce according to Grandma Jenkins; never disagree with the hand that feeds you.

I clear my throat in an attempt to cut through the tension invading the room. "Thank you, Tom, I'll take it from here. Didn't you and Ella have an appointment to meet with that local producer we're interested in?"

Tom frowns and glances at his ever-present cell phone. "In half an hour. We'll be cutting it close *now*." He sends another squint-eyed look at Rhys as though it's his fault. "I better go and see if Ella's over her… mood swing."

Irritated, I let him go without the usual pleasantries. Tom is the youngest child in a large, boisterous family, and as such expects the world to revolve around him. On the other hand, he's generous to a fault, normally even-tempered, and loves Ella to death. I can forgive him for his chauvinism if he doesn't hurt my friend—or my company.

I catch Rhys' speculative gaze and raise a brow, daring him to comment but it's like he reads my mind because he changes the subject.

"How long have you lived here?"

I stare at him, surprised. "In Seattle? Most of my life. I grew up near the Elliott Bay Marina. My grandmother has… had, a craftsman cottage and a twenty-seven-foot Catalina. She raised me with a love of the water." And I'd taken those days for granted. The Memories of weekend trips up and down the coast, the wind in our sails and sheer joy filling our hearts is sorely missed. I'd do anything to get them back.

"She sold them?" Rhys asked, seemingly genuinely curious.

My throat tightens. "Not quite. She passed away six months ago. I live alone in the house and have been contemplating selling the boat. It's too big for one person to comfortably handle."

Rhys shifts in his seat and I give him an embarrassed smile. "Guess you weren't looking for my life history. I tend to talk too much when I'm nervous, you'll get used to it."

"I didn't mean to upset you. My father would be the first to preach about keeping it professional. I'm sorry." He stands and does up his jacket. "I'll take these to the hotel and go over them there. Tomorrow I want to pay a visit to the warehouse. Is there someone available to walk through it with me?"

Tom or Ella could easily guide him around our state-of-art packaging complex, but I practically hop out of my seat. "I'm free. Do you want to do breakfast first?" Then, in case he thinks I'm asking him out on a date, "We can drop in on one of my suppliers along the way."

Rhys hesitates, then seems to gird his loins, so to speak. "As long as you don't take me onto any elevators or dump breakfast in my lap, you have a deal."

Well, if he fails to save my business, he could get a job as a comedian.

6

Rhys

Unlike the first time we met, Georgina arrives in front of my hotel promptly at eight with not a hair out of place or damp spot to be found. I know this because I have a hard time keeping my eyes off her as she expertly drives her sporty little hatchback through the morning commute. The dark skirt she has on is slitted up the side, allowing me glimpses of creamy smooth-looking skin every time she lifts a wedged heel to work the pedals. A white dress shirt gapes between her generous breasts, teasing me with the dainty lace of her bra, and if her fingers brush my thigh one more time as she shifts gears, I can't be held accountable for my actions.

"Hot?" she asks as I roll my window halfway down, breathing in the brisk spring air.

I shoot her a glare, sure she's playing me, but no, her attention seems to be solely focused on the traffic, though there's a suspicious little twitch to her luscious pink lips. Great, now I'm staring at her mouth. Maybe I needed more sleep last night and less late-night television.

"Had your license long?" I counter as she blows through a yellow light.

She chuckles and shifts lanes, narrowly avoiding a collision with the rear-end of a garbage truck. "Only since I was sixteen. Grandma Jenkins taught me how to drive." She glances at me with a smile that could melt snow.

"Eyes on the road," I warn as a Beemer slows in front of her.

"Are you one of those backseat drivers?" she says, already in the midst of hitting the brake.

I could tell her my mom died because of a careless driver, but for some reason, I don't. I can see she loves being behind the wheel and I don't want to take that away from her. We'll probably never ride in the same vehicle again, anyway.

"Something like that," I murmur and change the subject. "I started on those reports you gave me last night. There are a few things I'd like to go over with you, but for the most part, they seem accurate."

"Gee, thanks," she mutters, grinding a gear.

I cringe and try not to imagine what those pink nails could do to me if she's annoyed. I'd much rather think of them clawing my back in pleasure, but that's not likely to happen any time soon. "What I mean is, the bookkeeping is better than I expected. Quite often, when a company is in trouble, we find the books are a mess."

"So, I can do my books but not run a business, is that what you're trying to imply?" she snaps, an ornery glint darkening jade-green eyes behind the heavy black frames of her glasses.

"Quit putting words in my mouth," I retort as she slams on the brakes just in time to stop for the next yellow light—shocker. "Many businesses are suffering through the economic downturn; you have nothing to be embarrassed about."

Her chest heaves, threatening the button between her breasts working valiantly to keep her decently covered. "You, you... jerk. I am *not* embarrassed, as you so creatively put it, I'm angry. Spitting mad, really." She jams the shifter into first. Her fingernails scrape my leg and send an electric shock north. I cover my crotch before she notices and thinks I'm some kind of pervert who gets off on quarreling.

I sigh my relief as she wheels into a busy restaurant parking lot. I wait until she finds a stall, pulls in and parks, before saying anything else. "Look, you're going to need tougher skin if you want to succeed in the business world."

Her car coughs when she turns the key off. The subsequent silence—other than the muted laughter and conversation from people walking past who actually want to be together—is uncomfortable.

Georgina stares out the front windshield, hands clenched in her lap. "I need this to work," she says quietly. "My parents loaned me the startup money to get *Bloomin' Right's* doors open. If I fail..." She swipes at a rogue tear with trembling fingers. "There's a lot on the line."

I gaze at her, lost for words. Doesn't she realize she'd gotten in bed with the devil when she partnered with my father? He gives loan sharks a bad name.

She turns to look at me, her eyes luminous. "Sorry, I didn't mean to unload on you, just... I know the stakes are high, so don't belittle my efforts, okay?"

I nod, chastised. "You're correct, of course. I have no right to jump to conclusions. That's why I'm here, to learn from you and hopefully work together to make *Bloomin' Right* the successful company it deserves to be."

She holds out her hand. "Start again?"

My chest tightens as I accept her peace offering. The sexual attraction I can deal with, this tug on the heartstrings though... I didn't expect to come here and get caught up in the lives of those I plan to ruin.

Damn my father to hell.

***

The inside of the family restaurant is as busy as the parking lot suggested, and we're forced to wait for seating. I would be impatient with the delay, except room in the short entry is at a premium and I end up with Georgina all but plastered to my body. The top of her silky brown hair—done up in a French braid today—tickles my chin, while her rounded butt nestles my dick. I start doing mathematical equations in my big head to keep my little head under control.

"Georgie, why didn't you tell me you were here?" A tall dude wearing an apron that says, '*Kiss me, I'm the chef*' strides through the crowd—actually the crowd parts like the Red Sea for him—and tugs Georgina forward into his massive arms. Being a typical girl, she giggles, and I have to stifle the urge to roll my eyes. And punch his nose.

After what feels like millennia, he lets her go and steps back to eye her from head to toe. "You're looking all dressed up today, *ma chérie.*" His flirtatious smile slowly vanishes as he takes me in. "Are you two-timing *moi*?" He says it like a joke, the arrogant...

"Paul, quit teasing." Georgina pats his chest, her

fingers lingering on his pec. "This is Mr. Turner, my new business partner."

I guess we're back to formalities. I nod at chef dude and look hopefully for a table. Time to wrap up this little *soirée*. "We're in a bit of a hurry, so..."

He smirks at me, well aware of my ploy. "Of course. There's always room for my favorite customer. Angela," he calls the server guiding people to their seats. "Take care of Georgie for me, *s'il vous plaît?*" He bends his head to brush her cheek with his lips. "I must get back to my kitchen."

"Talk to you later?" Georgina asks, as though she can't stand to let him go.

I'm beginning to feel like a third wheel, and I don't like it. I don't have time for someone's romantic entanglements. It's got nothing to do with my own attraction to the fiery brunette. The sooner I get her business in tip-top shape and sell it, the better off we'll all be.

If only I can make myself believe my own hogwash.

7

Georgina

I anxiously watch Rhys push the food around his plate, and hope he's simply distracted. There's a lot riding on the taste and presentation of the fare set out before us. Paul went all out, bless his soul, creating culinary masterpieces for our guest.

Except, he's not eating.

I clear my throat and timidly venture, "Something wrong with the food?"

He glances up, a distracted look on his too-handsome-for-comfort face, before setting his fork down and using the cloth napkin provided to brush his lips. *Lucky napkin.*

"The meal is fine," he says. "Your... friend is an excellent cook."

"Chef," I reply automatically. "Paul went to the

Institute of Culinary Education in New York. He's rightfully proud of his achievements."

Rhys lifts a brow and takes another look around the crowded restaurant. I know what he sees; a family establishment, big on casual dining instead of the sleek and sophisticated décor most Michelin trained chefs prefer. That's not Paul though, he wants to stay true to his roots. I admire that.

A server in the standard uniform of black shirt and pants goes past with a tray of breakfast dishes. The mouthwatering aroma of smoky bacon and waffles piled high with a fresh berry compote teases my nostrils though I'm so full I'm in danger of waddling out of here. What a day to choose a pencil skirt; my stomach is revolting.

"Paul smokes his own meat and has a rooftop garden that he uses for herbs and vegetables. He prides himself on growing as much organic produce as he can, and when he can't, he sources it locally. You can literally taste the difference with his food."

"I take it you're a fan." Rhys says with a touch of sarcasm, his blue eyes mocking.

What does it take to impress this guy?

"He's worked hard to make a name for himself. He comes from a humble background. Life wasn't easy, but that didn't stop him from going after his dreams. Paul may be my cousin, but he's also one of the best men I know." I relax tense muscles and sit back, embarrassed to realize I'd practically pounced down Rhys' throat.

He holds up a hand in peace, a slow smile curving his lips. "Whoa there, She-Ra. Your cousin is lucky to have you on his side. So, tell me how he fits into your project."

I breathe out a relieved sigh, grateful he's at least willing to listen to my ideas. "We've always had strong ethics at *Bloomin' Right,* making sure our wholesome products are delivered fresh to our customers' doors, but it isn't enough to make us stand out from our competitors."

I take a second to gather my thoughts and enjoy the robust flavor of the coffee on my tongue. "I knew we needed to go in another direction, but had a tough time coming up with the concept—until now."

Rhys sips his drink and nods. "That's where we come in."

"Yes." CLO is my last chance to keep *my* dream alive. Maybe that, as much as anything, drove me to ask for help. Paul offered to lend me the finances to implement my new strategy, but I've borrowed enough from my family—too much—it's time I handle things on my own.

I take a deep breath before diving into my plan. If I can't sell Rhys on its validity, he has the power to override my wishes and take the company in whatever direction he chooses. Once again, I pray giving away fifty-one percent of *Bloomin' Right* isn't a mistake I'll live to regret.

"Families are becoming more and more focused on healthier food choices, whether at home or when they eat out.

"As you can see," I spread an enveloping arm to encompass the busy restaurant, "Paul is putting that concept into practice with great success. I've teamed up with him to provide fresh, organic herbs and produce for our meal kits. As well, we're working on dessert recipes we could include for an extra fee. I'd like to purchase anything Paul can't provide through local Farmers' Markets and use that as a promotional feature.

"Additionally, I'm currently in talks with a nearby meat market to line up weekly deliveries of organic free-range chicken, pork, and beef. With high quality foods and our easy-to-follow recipes, I believe we could pick up a wider consumer base."

"Yes, but at what cost?" Rhys cut in just as our server arrives with fresh coffee.

"Is there anything else I can get for you?" she asks, smiling coyly at Rhys while gathering our dirty dishes.

"Just the bill, thank you," I say with saccharine sweetness.

"Oh," she exclaims, losing the flirty look. "Paul

said, 'Don't even think of letting my cousin pick up the bill.' I guess that must be you."

My smile is genuine this time. "Tell him I owe him one."

She nods and hurries away, the tray of dishes resting comfortably shoulder high.

My gaze returns to our table and I see Rhys watching me with somber eyes. The breakfast I'd enjoyed a moment ago rolls around unpleasantly in my stomach. I know that look. It's one I've seen many times over the years.

"You're going to say no, aren't you?" Might as well pull the bandage off. It's going to hurt whether I wait or do it now and get it over with. Years of my hard work are about to be turned into a commercial enterprise.

He taps the table with his fingers and stares at his coffee cup as though it holds the answers. I could tell him it won't work. I've spent many hours doing the same without any eureka-type moments.

Instead, he surprises me.

"I'd need to see a detailed plan. Everything." He pins me with a laser-blue gaze. "Costs, projected profit, labor, shipping, every detail needs to be taken into consideration before I'm willing to take this to the CLO board of directors. You get me what I need, and I'll see what I can do—no guarantees."

Stunned that I'd won this round, I stare at the man

who holds my future in his hands and a smile so wide it hurts my cheeks takes over my face.

It's not over after all.

***

I shiver as a blast of cold air hits us the moment we step through the heavy steel door leading into *Bloomin' Right's* distribution center. A short hall leads to the main warehouse. Banks of walk-in coolers run along the left wall and subzero freezers line the right. The rest of the cavernous space is taken up with rows of metal shelving filled with a variety of dry goods; big bags of jasmine rice, cavatappi noodles, boxes of beans, tomatoes, corn, couscous, farro, individual packets of mayonnaise, red wine vinegar, honey, jam, and spices. Everything required to complete the recipes my team works so hard to put together.

A forklift zooms by with a loaded pallet. The driver nods, his head covered by a shiny yellow hard hat, and eyes the stranger in our midst. I'm grateful Ella is an organization freak and keeps the building impeccably clean.

"This place is larger than I expected." Rhys turns in a slow circle taking it all in.

"We need the space," I say, defending my choice. "Our customer base is growing. We have orders going out Monday through Friday, and deliveries to the warehouse on Saturday. I currently staff twelve full-time workers and five part-time students."

"That's another thing we need to talk about," Rhys says, focusing on me. "You have too many employees for the size of your business. By the time you cover payroll, taxes, employment insurance, and workers' compensation you're driving your profits into the red."

"Tell me what you really think," I mutter sarcastically.

He shrugs. "I wouldn't be doing my job if I didn't point out deficiencies. If we work together to tighten your expenses, we can gain a substantial profit margin."

"I'm *not* letting my crew go, so forget it," I snap.

"Stalemate." He points to a room where people are coming and going with carts filled with food items. "What's going on there?"

My excitement at showing him the hub of our company has dimmed, but I lead him toward the testing room.

"Georgina, just in time. Come check this out." Sara, one of my meal designers, stands in front of one of three industrial stoves, blowing on a spoon.

"Is this the sauce you were talking about?" I ask, joining her to grab a sample of my own.

"Yes. Cherry jam, fried onions, and chili peppers. What do you think?"

I taste it and tears form. “Hot,” I breathe out around the fumes.

“I like spicy. Mind if I try?” Rhys grins at my discomfort.

Sara looks askance at me, then hands him a spoon and steps out of his way. I watch and wait, half-hoping he burns his tongue. He takes a careful sip, licks his lips, and nods approvingly.

“This is good—really good. I’m impressed.” He turns the full wattage of his smile on poor Sara and she’s lost, putty in his clever hands.

“Thank you,” she gushes, sending a reproving glance my way. I shrug, unrepentant. My mouth is still on fire. “This would be the perfect accompaniment with pork or chicken. You can set the heat for those with delicate constitutions with the amount of chili pepper used.”

Like me.

I reach into the cupboard for a glass and stride to the water cooler, intent on dousing the flames. A thump jiggles the box by my foot. I screech and jump backward, spilling water on the floor.

“What *is* that?” I stare at the box in horror.

Sara rushes over with a wad of paper towels in hand and drops to her knees to clean up the mess while sending me a contrite look. “I’m so sorry, Georgina, I knew it wasn’t a good idea, but he’s just so—”

Rhys carefully lifts the lid as she's explaining and a fuzzy brown face peers up at us.

"A puppy," Rhys and I announce at the same time, scaring the poor thing. It lets out a frightened yip and cowers in the corner, tail between its legs.

I crouch down and let the pup smell my hand before ruffling soft ears tipped in black. "Is she/he yours, Sara?" I sneak a glance at Rhys, expecting a disapproving frown, but he surprises me by stealing a few scraps of beef off a plate on the counter and offering it to the dog.

"What?" he asks, catching my look. "It's skin and bone." His lips quirk when the pup sniffs, then delicately accepts the offering. "Must be female, she has manners."

That startles a laugh out of me. He keeps surprising me. It's hard to hate a guy with a nice streak.

"I found him hiding in the bushes out front this morning," Sara says, throwing the wet towels into the trash before washing her hands. She looks at me with apologetic eyes. "It's just for today. I'll take him—her—to the pound right after work, I promise."

I stare into limpid brown eyes and know I can't let that happen. "I'll take him home with me," I say, surprising Rhys and Sara. I rub the silky head one more time, then rise and shoulder my purse. "Temporarily, of course. She'll be comfortable at Grandma Jenkins' until we find a family for her.

"But," I add, "next time, call me first. This is a health violation. We could get closed down for an infraction like this. You know the rules, Sara." I smile a little to ease the reprimand.

Sara nods, her cheeks flushed. "Of course. Thank you, Georgina."

I give her a quick hug. "You did the right thing."

Rhys sets the lid on the box and lifts it into his arms. "Ready?"

"I am. Thanks, Rhys. Sorry to cut the tour short." I check the box for air holes and lead the way out. "I'll need to stop at a pet store on the way. Want dropped at your hotel?"

Rhys cradles the box and looks at me over the top. "I was thinking I could give you a hand. That way we can collaborate on a marketing strategy at the same time."

I reluctantly nod and open the car door so he can set the pup on the backseat. And I thought puppy pads would be my biggest worry today.

8

Rhys

I volunteer to wait in the car with the pup while Georgina runs into the pet store for the essentials. I plan on using the time to catch up on emails, but instead, end up watching her walk across the parking lot in that breath-stealing skirt. I'm not the only one who notices, either. A couple of exec-types leave the coffee shop next door to the pet store and pause to bestow charming smiles on her. One even hurries over to open the door—

"She doesn't even realize how attractive she is," I murmur as she tucks her hair behind her ear and awkwardly returns the guy's smile. The pup whimpers in reply.

I wait until Georgina disappears from view—and the men go separate ways—before turning in my seat to lift the lid on the box. The pup looks up at me with woebegone eyes.

"Where's your momma, little one?" I give in and lift her—it's a girl—into my arms. "You're a scrawny thing, aren't you?"

Happy to be out of confinement, she scrambles up my chest and lick/bites my chin, giving me a kiss with her puppy breath.

"Whoa there, Buttercup, settle down now." I huff out a chuckle and lower her to my lap. "You can't be much more than eight or nine weeks old. Too young to be on your own." I pet her bony back and my heart twists. How can people be so cruel? Maybe it's because I only ever had one dog—back before Mom died and our family along with her—but this pipsqueak draws out my protective instincts. I'm almost tempted to keep Buttercup myself, but it wouldn't be fair to her. My life is one hotel room after another. Business meeting after business meeting. I don't have time to turn around, never mind care for a puppy.

"Sorry, little one. Don't worry, Georgina will find you a good home." *I hope.*

My cell phone rings in my pocket, startling both of us. I hold the pup to the side and pull the thing out, my gut telling me who it is before I even see the name on the screen.

"Hello, Father." I grimace and rub Buttercup's soft fur for comfort.

"Rhys. I've been expecting to hear from you, Son. The board wants a report."

Yes, I arrived safe and sound. Thanks for your concern. "I'm aware of that, Dad. I've only been here a couple of days, hardly enough time to reach a conclusion." I glare at the cars moving in and out of the parking lot, until a woman pushing a stroller notices and picks up speed to escape my death ray. I lower my gaze to Georgina's cracked dash and sigh. "I'll have more to tell you by the end of the week."

"The end of the—?"

"Friday, Dad. That's the best I can do."

It's my father's turn to let out a gusty sigh. "Well, I'm sure that will be fine. The faster the turnaround, the better, but I don't have to tell you that. Is the owner cooperative? If not, use your leverage, boy. That's how big business works."

At the cost of people's livelihoods. I know all about it. Speak of the debutante... "Gotta go, Father. I'll have my findings to you by Friday." I hang up and hurry to set the pup back in the box, then hop out to give Georgina a hand with her bags.

"Did you buy out the store?" I ask, my voice snarky, a carryover from the conversation with my dad. I hoist a chenille dog bed under one arm and a big bag of grain free—written in large letters—food in the other.

Her glasses are foggy from the exertion of getting all the packages out of the store, but I still feel the chill of her sarcasm. "Not quite. I left the doghouse for you."

Zing.

The call with my father fades away. I grin and follow her to the wreck she calls a car. The parking lot is crowded, forcing me to put the food in the bed, lift the whole thing over my head, and slide sideways to the back of the car where she already has the trunk open and is rearranging a pile of... stuff, so we can unload our parcels.

"You should have a truck," I mutter, cramming the dog food into a corner. I bang my head on the trunk lid and curse as I straighten.

"There's no need to swear, I didn't ask you for help." Georgina crosses her arms under full breasts and eyes the red mark I must have on my head as though I've done it on purpose.

"God forbid. Why is it that women always expect men to do things for them, but they refuse to come right out and ask us, and then get upset when we don't pick up on the signs?" I rub the sore spot and slam the trunk closed with a satisfying bang.

"Why should we have to? If men paid attention, the world would be a better place." Satisfied she'd gotten the last word in, Georgina sashays to the driver's side and opens the car door. I hear a startled cry, then she drops to the ground.

Holy shit, is she having a heart attack? My own heart leapfrogging out of my chest, I race around the back of the car, my feet feeling as though they're weighted by sandbags, only to find Georgina's shapely butt in the air and her arm under the vehicle parked next to ours, a SUV with black running boards.

"What are you...?" *Oh, no.* Upset from the conversation with my father, I hadn't replaced the lid on Buttercup's box.

I fall to my knees behind Georgina and try to get a look under the SUV. "Did you see which way she went?" I ask, my mouth going dry.

Her butt waves in my face as Georgina shifts to glance back at me, eyes wide. "Hurry, run to the other side before she gets away. She's behind the front tire."

Not wasting another second, I jump to my feet and sprint to the driver's side of the SUV, praying the traffic stays away. Nightmare visions of the tiny pup ending up beneath the wheels of a car turn my stomach inside out.

I roll onto my back and edge under the vehicle, doing my best to ignore the claustrophobia tightening my chest. Pebbles dig into my skin and an oily aroma warns me I've probably ruined another shirt since taking on this project, but none of that matters when I catch sight of Buttercup. She's shivering and shaking, huddled against the dirty tire rim, her sandy brown fur mussed and dark with oil from the stain on the pavement.

"Come on, Buttercup. That's a good girl. Come on, sweetheart. It's okay, we've got you." I stretch out my fingers and hold my breath, hoping she trusts my scent enough to come to me rather than making a dash into the parking lot.

Long moments pass as vehicles roll by, taking my breath with their spinning tires. I don't dare look at Georgina, her tears would ruin me.

"Please come out, Buttercup. I'll never complain about carrying your sh... stuff again."

A muffled laugh perks up the pup's drooping ears. "I'm holding you to that," Georgina says.

I take a gamble and glance at her anyway, I can't help myself. Sure enough, her eyes are bright, and incredibly beautiful. They capture me with their brilliance and send my pulse skittering like lightning bugs in a midnight sky.

"Oh, she's moving," Georgina whispers, practically exploding with excitement.

I jerk my attention back to Buttercup and sure enough, she's crawling on four paws toward my fingers, one excruciating inch at a time. "That's it, baby. Just a little bit more and we can get out from under this stinky undercarriage. My guess is you're in for a bath when we get home. Don't blame me, you're the one who rolled around in that greasy puddle. You owe me a shirt, by the way." I keep up a steady dialogue, hoping the pup recognizes me and senses I would never hurt her.

Finally, I feel her wet nose on my skin, then her warm belly as she skitters down the length of my arm to kiss/lick my face again. Nothing ever felt so good.

I sit up with her in my arms, scared to squeeze her the way I want to. "That was too close."

Georgina appears, hands fluttering. "Is she okay? I was so scared..."

I rise and stride toward her like a superhero, the pup cuddled against my chest. "She's fine. Unlike my shirt." I roll my shoulder to show her the wet stain.

"Serves you right," she says, holding her hands out for the dog. "Did you leave the lid off the box? When I think what could have happened—"

"But didn't," I point out, striving to remain calm. I deserve her rancor, but she has to admit I've saved the day—doesn't she?

She kisses the top of Buttercup's head, then gently sets her in the box and deliberately replaces the lid before straightening to look at me with a raised brow. "I'm taking the pup home for a bath.

You can find your way to your hotel from here, I assume?"

Okay, maybe not. "Sure, whatever. I'll call you later then?" Geez, now I sound like a discarded boyfriend. "We still have those files to go over."

She climbs behind the wheel and rolls down her window. "Do you like spaghetti?"

My foolish heart rises like a helium balloon. "Who doesn't?" I say with a goofy grin.

"My place, six o'clock. Bring some wine, I have a feeling it's going to be a long night." With that she fires up her engine and pulls out of the lot.

It's only after she's gone that I realize my phone is in her car.

Some superhero.

9

Georgina

By the time I get Buttercup home—I didn't tell Rhys, but I like the name he chose for the pup—I'm ready for a nap. Instead, I cart all my four-legged guest's bags into the house, then go back to the car for the dog.

"Okay, Buttercup, I hope you like Grandma Jenkins' house." I carry the box into the foyer and set it carefully down. When I lift the lid, my heart goes to mush. She looks at me with the saddest eyes I've ever seen. Dirty, dark patches mar her straw-colored coat, and one ear flops adorably inside out, like an antenna caught in a windstorm.

"You're not going to be impressed, but a bath seems to be first on our list." I gingerly pick her up around the body and hold her away from my clothes. Of course, she panics, her stubby legs doggy paddling in the air.

Thank goodness we aren't going far. The bathroom on the main floor is situated under the stairs and boasts a gorgeous clawfoot tub. I snag the dog shampoo out of the top of a bag on my way and a snow-white towel from the rack, grimacing at the thought of the grease stains I'll likely never get out, and lay it in the bottom of the tub before setting the pup down. It's probably a good idea to use the shower head for adding water instead of the gushing waterfall that comes from the tap. I don't want to freak her out any worse than she is —poor girl.

I kneel on the floor and lay the shower head on its side, facing away from Buttercup, put my hand on her back, and turn on the water, setting the temperature to lukewarm. It doesn't take long before her fur is floating on the water like one of the kelp beds that line the waterways. I use my hand to cup water and gently pour it over her back.

"Aw." I chuckle. "You look like a drowned rat." Buttercup looks up at me and blinks, her body quivering. "Don't be scared, I won't let anything happen to you. Just wait, you'll be the prettiest dog on the block by the time we're through." I have a feeling she's happy the way she is.

I'm not exactly sure what I'm doing, but I try not to

get soap in her eyes, and other than that, go about the process much the same as washing my own hair. "I've never had a puppy before, so bear with me, okay?" Buttercup sneezes, her wet lashes stuck together. "Oops, bless you," I say, grinning. "It's not my fault. My parents have busy careers. Dad's a biology professor and Mom is a high school counselor, they met at university."

I reach behind me for a dry towel and pull the plug in the bathtub before lifting Buttercup out and onto my lap. "Anyway, there was barely time for me, never mind caring for pets, so..." I rub her down, laughing at the comical picture she makes, her hair sticking up as though filled with static electricity. "You're it."

As though she knows of the children's game of *Tag*, Buttercup squiggles free of my grasp, shakes so hard she topples over, scrambles back up again, then bolts from the room, her nails clicking on the hardwood flooring.

"Shoot," I cry, clambering to my feet to give chase. "Buttercup, come back here, you little pipsqueak." The good news; no steps for her to fall, though there is a set of stairs leading to the second floor and the bedrooms. The bad news; there are literally hundreds of spots a puppy could hide in.

I follow the damp trail until it disappears, then begin the time-consuming process of looking around or under every piece of Grandma Jenkins' antique furniture. Not under the armoire, or the rolled arm sofa in a lush mocha brown. I lift the skirt on Grandma's favorite slipcovered armchair, expecting to find a pair of brown eyes staring back at me, but no such luck.

Now what? I can't very well tell Rhys I lost the dog right after he saved it. I glance at the cuckoo clock on the wall—Grandma found it at a yard sale and fell in love with it—and realize I only have a couple of hours until he arrives for dinner. Unless he stands me up. I couldn't really blame the guy, considering I left him standing in a parking lot in a strange city. If my goal is to prove how unprofessional I can act, I'm doing a fine job. Which is why tonight I'm pulling out all the stops. I invited Rhys to a spaghetti dinner and that's what he's going to get—with a twist.

"Okay, you win. I'm going for a shower. Come out when you're ready." I stand and move toward the bathroom but make a slight detour to lay a puppy pad down in a conspicuous place. "Be a good girl and use this to do your business, please."

I rush through the shower, concerned I might come out to a half-eaten sofa—never mind the fact Buttercup could hardly make the leap.

Wrapped in a bath towel like a mummy, I waddle toward my bedroom—converted from the formal dining room that I would never use—keeping an eye out for any surprise packages. So far, so good. My door is open and the moment I step into the room, I freeze. Buttercup is curled into a little brown ball on top of my favorite wool sweater that *somehow* fell off the rocking chair sitting in the alcove.

"There you are," I whisper, creeping across to the closet. Of course, the door creaks and the pup wakes with a whimper and a yawn. Her fur is wavy now and looks impossibly soft to the touch.

"I bet you're hungry, aren't you?" I start to dig out some clothes, willing Buttercup to go back to sleep, but no such luck. She gets up, shakes her head hard enough to make both ears flop backward, stretches, and does her imitation of a bloodhound, sniffing my sweater and the surrounding carpet.

"What are y—" I catch her starting to squat and let out a little squeak. "No, you don't." I race over, pick her up, and double-time it down the hall to the puppy pad. We make it just in time and I clap and cheer like a lunatic. "Good girl. You're so smart. What a good puppy." Totally ignoring the fact she almost peed on my favorite sweater.

Buttercup looks up at me, tail wagging, as though she knows she's accomplished a miracle, and gives a joyful little bark.

I laugh. "Yes, you're a wonder dog. Let's go and

find you a well-deserved treat, and then I really need to get some clothes on."

I look through the first bag and find the adorable pink jewel-studded collar I couldn't resist in the store, and black and white checkered dog dishes with paw prints embedded in the bottom of the bowls. Buttercup whines and I hurry to the next bag. Who knows how long it's been since the poor thing had a decent meal? I finally find the bag of way-too-expensive puppy food, recommended to me by the clerk at the pet store, just as the doorbell rings.

Startled, I look from the door to the cuckoo clock and back to the door. That can't be Rhys, can it? The bell blares again as though whoever is on the other side has their finger glued to the darn thing.

Annoyed, I stomp to the door and swing it open. Sure enough, it's my pain-in-the-butt CEO. "You're early," I snap.

And you're..." He takes a leisurely tour of my body from head to toe and ends on my breasts. "Naked."

10

Rhys

I'm almost certain my eyes are bugging out of my head. I think I've swallowed my tongue and I *know* my mouth is hanging open, but it's not every day I'm greeted at the door by a half-naked temptress.

"I'm *not* naked," Georgina huffs, threatening the towel precariously knotted between her breasts. "Would you *please* take this to the kitchen and feed the dog while I get dressed?" She's rosy from chest to cheeks but lifts her chin and holds out a bag of kibble and a couple of girly bowls.

"Don't get dressed on my account," I say, juggling the bottle of wine I brought with the bag she thrusts into my arms. "I didn't realize this was going to be a casual affair."

She shoots me a '*get real*' look and turns away,

affording me an appetizing view of the backs of her thighs below the towel. "First, there will be no affairs, casual or otherwise, and secondly if you hadn't arrived three quarters of an hour early, I would have been ready. Did you follow me from the pet store?"

Reminded of her less than gracious attitude earlier, the lascivious thoughts I've been entertaining return to a simmer. "Do you realize I had to beg a stranger for the use of his phone in order to call a cab? And *then*, it took them forty-five minutes to get there. That's going to cost you, Ms. Michaels." I mean an extra helping of dessert, but she obviously takes it as something else.

She whirls around and glares at me, her eyes full of righteous indignation, and something I couldn't quite put my finger on—fear, maybe? It makes me want to punch the asshole who put those memories there.

I open my mouth to apologize for the misconception, but she beats me to it, though not in a way I expect.

The strong visage I've come to associate with Georgina disappears, leaving a shell of the person behind. "I'm sorry, this is a bad idea. If you don't mind, I think you should go."

I won't stay where I'm not wanted. It was a mistake to come here, to her home, anyway. We're nothing more than work associates, and even that is temporary. Much better to keep our relationship to that of strangers. Though she doesn't *feel* like a stranger to me. She's... more.

"Sure," I say, carefully setting the dog food and wine on the navy hall tree bench just inside the door. The last thing I want is to make her uncomfortable in her own home. "I just need my phone back so I can call the taxi service."

"Your phone...?" She stares at me, puzzled. Then the light comes on and she gasps. "That's right. You left your phone in my car while we chased Buttercup. No wonder you had to ask a stranger for help." She giggles and it fizzles in my chest.

"You named her Buttercup?" I ask, touched.

She shrugs one smooth, kissable shoulder. "She likes it." Her soft smile suggests she does, too.

"It suits her," I murmur, unwilling to break the tenuous bond formed by one small pup. "Well, I better make that call so I can get out of your hair."

"Oh, yes, of course." She moves toward me, her bare feet with their blue and pink candy-striped nails sending me right back into fantasyland again. Who would have guessed I had a hidden foot fetish?

"I'll just get my keys," she whispers, stretching for the purse sitting next to where I'd set down the bottle of wine.

"Let—" I reach for the bag at the same time, startling Georgina, who jerks back and bumps the bottle.

We both watch in horror as it rocks before toppling to the floor with an ominous crack and shards of glass and liquid spill from of the neck.

"Don't move," I snap, visions of glass piercing soft skin turning my stomach.

"*Don't* yell at me," she retorts, stamping her foot.

Terrified, I scoop her into my arms. "Are you *crazy*? You just broke a bottle. On the floor. Where you were stomping your *bare* feet."

When she doesn't freak out at my abrupt treatment, I look into her face and still. "What?"

Her eyes are mesmerizing, a deep emerald green with a ring of golden brown around the iris. I suddenly realize she's not wearing her glasses. "How well can you see without your specs?" No wonder she'd acted carelessly, she probably couldn't see the splinters of glass or the wine dribbling onto the floor.

"I don't need to see to feel your arms around me," she says in a hushed voice. "What are you doing?"

She fits in my arms as though she's meant to be there. One hand cradles her ribs, right under the full breasts that haunt my dreams, and the other hand is in nirvana, wrapped around a silky-smooth thigh.

"Saving your life," I breathe, before lowering my lips to hers. The first touch sends a shock of desire straight to my groin. I groan and deepen the connection, my fingers spreading to take in as many sensations as I can. Georgina utters a hungry sound and lifts her arms to grasp my head, holding me in place for her nibbling teeth and foraging tongue.

"We need to stop," she gasps, her fingers clenched in my hair.

Her scent, her touch, everything about Georgina Michaels calls to me on an elemental level. "Soon," I murmur, intent on nudging her towel loose so I can taste the skin that's been driving me crazy.

Her breast is as lush and beautiful as I'd expected, and I take a moment to imprint it on my befuddled brain before leaning down to suckle the rosy nipple into my mouth. Her fingers flex on my scalp, causing erotic shivers to cascade down my spine straight to my dick. My body is thrumming with enough pheromones to burn the house down.

"I want you," I mutter, starting down the hall toward what I hope is her bedroom.

"I want you, too, but..."

The hesitation in her voice slows me in my tracks. I may be an asshole, but I don't force a woman to do something she's not ready for.

With a last regret-filled kiss, I set her on her feet and gently pull up the towel, covering her flushed breast. "But, it's too soon." I keep my hands on her arms, unwilling to completely break contact just yet.

She nods, her eyes downcast. "I'm sorry, Rhys. It's

not you." She glances up with a mischievous twinkle, though I see that hint of pain again. "Well, it's partly you. We've argued since we met, and that's not even taking into consideration our professional relationship."

"But," I counter, brushing a length of damp, wavy brown hair behind her ear, "you can't deny the chemistry between us. I want to get to know you better, Georgina Michaels."

It's a mistake, I know that. My father is the fly in the ointment. He's not going to change his mind about *Bloomin' Right* unless I can prove it to be a viable business. When Georgina finds out we have no intention of helping her beyond fixing the books enough to sell at a profit, she'll never forgive me. I want to tell her, I *need* to tell her, but loyalty to the father who raised me and paid for my education stills my tongue.

Buttercup crawls out from under an ornate sofa table and I scoop her into my arms, needing the comfort. "Hello, sweetheart. You smell a lot better. Did Mommy give you a bath?" Listen to me, schmoozing a dog. Dad would be so proud.

"I did, and she took it like a champ," Georgina says, ruffling the fuzzy head.

I'm comfortable here in a way I haven't been since my mother died. I don't want to leave, but Georgina needs space, so I hand the pup to her and take a step back though it pains me to go.

"Stay here, I'll grab your purse and clean up that mess." I turn toward the hall tree, but Georgina's hand on my arm stops me.

"I've changed my mind. Will you have dinner with us?"

I stare at a set of brown puppy-dog eyes, and a set of mysterious green ones and am helpless to deny either of them. "I'd love to."

11

Georgina

I must be crazy. Why else would I invite a man I've only known for a handful of days into Grandma Jenkins' home? The place where I'd always been free to be *me*. There are bittersweet memories in every nook and cranny of this old house. Family photos cover the walls, keepsakes from Grandma's travels, old vases, and pieces of art passed down through the generations litter every table and curio cabinet.

It's personal, and Rhys is taking it all in with penetrating eyes that seem to see everything. Even the things I don't want him to see.

He's standing near the El Greco cream marble fireplace, staring at a watercolor I'd done after a voyage on the water with Grandma Jenkins when I come back from getting changed. It'd been shortly after Daniel...

Grandma insisted she needed help with the boat, but I knew what she was doing.

"The ocean heals the soul, child. No matter how bad life gets, a trip to the water will leave you restored —trust me."

I'm not sure how much the briny sea air had to do with it, but I did return from that vacation with a clearer head, and soon after sat down and painted Grandma's sailboat as a way to say thank you.

"She loved that boat," I say softly, the weight of loss tempered tonight by fond memories.

Rhys turns to me, his expression lacking the cynicism I've come to associate with him. "She must have been important to you."

"You have no idea," I say with a laugh. "For her seventieth birthday she went sky-diving. Mom and Dad wanted to get her tested for dementia. Grandma informed them that if she *was* losing her mind, at least she would do it on her terms, thank you very much. She was one of a kind."

"That explains a lot," he murmurs.

My brows do the downward dog scrunch. "What's that supposed to mean?"

He grins, happy he got my goat. "Just that I see a lot of your grandmother's spontaneity in you."

I think that over, looking for any underlying meanings, then decide to give him the benefit of the doubt. "I'll take that as a compliment. So, are you hungry?"

He rubs his stomach, drawing attention to taut abs outlined by the white button-down he's wearing with the sleeves rolled up to the elbows. A thrill runs through me at the memory of those strong arms holding me safe and secure against his chest. And those lips...

"Georgina, are you all right?"

Rhys' voice and his hand cupping my shoulder jerk me back to the present. "Yeah, sure," I say, turning away to walk into the kitchen and escape those knowing eyes. "I was just thinking about... something else. Hope you have some knife skills. I'm going to put you to work."

I'm proud of this kitchen. It's a blend of old and new in a classic style that suits the house. It's one of the few rooms—the bathroom being the other—that I managed to convince Grandma needed upgrading. It has turned out both beautiful and functional.

I use the pot filler on the wall behind the large six-burner gas stove to add water to a stainless-steel pasta pot and nod toward the oversized refrigerator. "There's garlic, onion, and tomatoes in there."

By the time he finds the vegetables and carries them to the sink to be rinsed, I have the pot heating and remove a heavy skillet from its storage spot in the oven to the top of the range. Buttercup has disappeared again after finishing her food and I give myself a mental reminder to track her down before bed to do her business. Hopefully, as she gets used to me, she'll quit feeling the need to hide.

"Okay, what's next?" Rhys brings a strainer filled with the rinsed vegetables to the quartz countertop on the kitchen island and sets it on a sheaf of paper toweling.

"You're being unusually helpful," I say, choosing a couple of sharp paring knives from the butcher-block.

"I have my moments," he replies, his brow rising at my sarcasm. "So, is this one of the recipes you use for your consumers?"

Chastised, I hand him a knife and reach for an onion—my least favorite vegetable to cut. "Yes. I wanted to show you how easy it is to create delicious homemade meals. Anyone can do it."

"Gee, thanks." He chooses a clove of garlic. "Needs to be peeled, I assume?"

"Here." I hold out my hand. "There's an easy way to strip the skin." I take the clove, set it on the cutting board, and lay the side of my knife on top. "Use the palm of your hand and hit the knife a couple of times like this—" I demonstrate, "and it'll come right off, see?"

Rhys nods his head, looking impressed. "Nice trick. Let me try..."

I watch to make sure he isn't going to cut himself, then go back to chopping my onion. We work companionably together and soon have a pile of veggies ready for the frying pan. The water is boiling, so I sprinkle a bit of sea salt and add a good handful of spaghetti to the pot.

Next, I turn on the pan, drizzle olive oil, and turn to Rhys. "You're next. Start with the onions. Let them cook on a medium-high heat until they become translucent, then turn down the heat and add the minced garlic and chopped tomatoes. Give it a stir and let it simmer while I grab a new bottle of wine."

"Yes, boss," he says with a wink before carrying the loaded cutting board to the stove.

I glance over my shoulder as I reach into the cupboard for glasses and my heart flutters. He looks right at home in my kitchen and that scares me to death.

12

Rhys

The kitchen smells like an Italian restaurant. My mouth waters as Georgina plates up our dishes from the stove and I uncork the wine with a soft plop.

"Cabernet Sauvignon, you have good taste." My business mind immediately makes the leap to adding wine pairing to the meal kits at an added expense. If CLO were keeping the business—which it's not.

Rather than allowing thoughts of my father to ruin my evening, I pour the wine and make a big production of breathing in the aromatic scent and swishing a bit in my mouth before swallowing with a satisfied nod. "Exquisite."

"Oh, so you're a wine connoisseur, as well? I'm impressed." Georgina set the steaming plates on the table and accepts a glass of the rich red wine.

"I'm a man of many talents." I tap my glass to hers in a toast. "Here's to our new... association."

"Cheers," she says, taking a sip with an enjoyable sigh. "I needed this."

"Do I stress you out?" I murmur, my attention on her moist lips.

She shrugs and takes a seat at the table. "There's a lot riding on our association—as you put it. I'm grateful your corporation is taking a chance on us. I don't want to let you down."

Oh, Georgina. Don't hedge all your bets on me. I'm bound to be the one to let you down.

Unwilling to spout trite lies, I join her at the table and pick up the tablespoon next to my plate. "Are you insulting my sauce?"

"Wha...?" She looks at me with a puzzled frown, then laughs. "No, silly. It's a trick Grandma Jenkins taught me. You take a forkful of spaghetti, like this—" she scoops up a helping of tomato encrusted pasta, "and roll the tines round and round in the bowl of the spoon. See? Nice and neat." She proceeds to take a big bite and her eyes close in rapture. "Mmm, that's good."

Her purr of pleasure rumbles through my chest with all the delicacy of a land mine. Erotic thoughts I have no business thinking heat my blood and drive my good intentions out the window.

"You have sauce..." I tap my mouth to show her

where and watch, fascinated, as she takes a swipe at the spot with the tip of her tongue.

"Better?" she asks, and if I didn't know better, I'd think she's flirting with me.

I give in to temptation and lean over to kiss the sauce away. "Delicious," I sigh, reluctantly returning to my seat.

"Hmm?" Her eyes are dazed. She drops the fork onto her plate with a slight clatter and tries to act as though nothing happened. "Oh, you mean the sauce. See what you can create with just a few fresh ingredients?"

"I'm suitably impressed," I agree. "But, Georgina, I wasn't talking about the food." There. Let her make what she wants of that. I lean back and sip my wine, gazing at her over my glass.

Flustered, she picks up her napkin and dabs her forehead. "Uhm, I don't know what to say."

I straighten. Suddenly, I feel like a pervert. "Forget I said that. It must be the wine." *Lame, Turner, you idiot.* "Tell me more about your process. How do you handle advertising? Do you have customer incentives? Loyalty rewards?"

"Rhys, slow down. You're giving me emotional whiplash." She pushes her dish aside and removes her glasses on the pretense of cleaning them. Maybe she's deciding whether to sue me for sexual harassment.

"I apologize. I always promised myself I'd never be that guy and yet, here we are." I clear my throat and look up at the ceiling with its solid wood crossbeams. "If you prefer to work with someone else, I can call one of my associates to take over here." I lower my gaze to hers. "It might be for the best."

Georgina shakes her head, lustrous chestnut hair brushing bare shoulders above her peasant top. "I don't want anyone else. We're a team. We survived a horrifying death together. You're stuck with me now." She smiles winningly and squeezes my hand. "Really, Rhys, don't go."

My throat tightens. I've never had anyone care if I stuck around or not. Even my dad. His only concern is what I can do for his corporation, he doesn't give a shit about me.

I turn my hand in hers and hold on. "You're one of a kind, do you know that?"

She flushes before gently pulling free. "There's nothing special about me, but I don't give up on my friends."

"Is that what I am, your friend?" My heart protests. The moment she sets that boundary between us, I know it's not enough. I want more from her; she's a bright ray of sunshine in the depressing gray of my life. I'm starving for her warmth and kindness.

She nods toward my untouched dinner. "Eat. You

need your strength to wash all those dishes we've created."

I chuckle. "Slave labor, huh? You drive a hard bargain. This really does look delicious." I take a bite and savor the combination of flavors. "Are you formally trained as a chef?"

She blushes at the compliment. "I've taken a few classes, but most of it is hands-on training with Grandma Jenkins. She loved to cook."

The love she had for her grandmother is palpable. And suddenly I know how her inspiration for the business came about.

"Was the name for the company your grandmother's idea?"

Her eyes grow bright and she reaches for her napkin. "It was her favorite saying. I think she fancied herself Australian." She laugh/sobs. "You would have liked her."

If she was anything like Georgina, I would have loved her. Now that I know her, I can't feature pulling the rug out from under her. But the only way I can *maybe* change my father's mind is to turn this company into profitable equity. Money talks in dear old Dad's world.

"I have a plan," I say with a surge of excitement. "We need to rebrand. Come back with an aggressive sales campaign. Streamline the menus. Lower our expenses and it might be possible to take your business to the next level. What do you say?"

She stares at me with disappointment darkening her eyes.

"No," she says, before getting up and walking away.

13

Georgina

Grandma Jenkins would be displeased. Her preaching rings in my ears. "Manners are like a pair of pants. You need to wear them out in public."

I thought Rhys understood. I don't know why I'm surprised his focus is on the bottom line—*my* focus should be there, too, but then I wouldn't need his help. Thing is, *Bloomin' Right* is Grandma. Her way of bringing our family together was by making cooking fun. It started me on this journey and now Rhys wants to suck the joy out of the process.

I close my bedroom door and sink onto the upholstered wooden rocking chair that's been passed down through four generations of women in our family. Buttercup yawns from the spot she's claimed on my sweater. I lift her up and bring her close for a commiserating cuddle. I love her sweet scent.

"Men suck," I mumble, planting a kiss on her fuzzy head. She licks me, tickling my palm, and curls onto my lap to go back to sleep. I envy her. I haven't had a peaceful snooze since I was forced to sell shares of my company. All I can do now is deal with it. Hopefully, my decision isn't going to bite me in the butt.

I should go out and see to my guest, but lean my head against the chair and close my eyes, instead. It feels as though I've been in overdrive forever. I'd hoped splitting responsibilities for the business would free me up to breathe again, but it's not going to happen with Rhys' plan. I have to fight him, of course. It's crazy. The only way I would consider any of it is if...

That's it.

I sit up straight, jostling poor Buttercup. What if we blend our ideas? I can see the logic in streamlining our menus—to a degree—and an aggressive ad campaign is much more in his wheelhouse than mine. I've dreamed of taking *Bloomin' Right* in a new direction for a long time, maybe this is my chance.

"Sorry, Buttercup, I have to go." I set her on my sweater with only a little twinge of regret that I'll probably never be able to wear it again, and hurry to fling the door open, then jump backward with a little cry. "Rhys, you startled me."

He stands in the hall, looking one part incredibly handsome and a whole lot miffed male. "Why did you run off like that?"

Because it's my modus operandi. I'd sooner hide from my problems than face them head on. I've almost scared him off already, though, so I think I'll keep that little nugget to myself for now.

"I needed to stretch after that big meal," I say noncommittally.

He looks at me doubtfully, well aware neither of us did the pasta justice.

"I've been thinking over what you said and decided you're right. We *do* need a better call to action plan, but it needs to be on my terms. I'm not willing to turn my business into some cookie cutter company with a healthy profit margin and absolutely no character. There has to be a way to compromise."

His gaze goes to my unmade bed and his shapely lips quirk. "Is that a hint?"

I glance over my shoulder, my stomach taking up residence in my throat. Sure enough, my plain white support bra is dangling off the bedpost from my harried dressing earlier. *Gah!*

I push my way through the doorway, forcing him to back up or get run over. At the moment, the last one has definite merit. "Let's take Buttercup for a walk. She needs the exercise, and I can share my ideas with you at the same time. You grab her leash and collar and I'll meet you in the living room."

"But..." he starts, the humor gone. "There's something I need—"

"Later," I interrupt, cutting him off before he can tempt me to see to all his needs. "Five minutes. In the den." I close the door with him on the other side and use my body as a bulwark, though why I think he's going to storm the barricade, I have no idea. It's not as though I'm a femme fatale—the opposite actually. Normally, a man like Rhys Turner wouldn't give me a second glance. So, is it a case of my vivid imagination, or is he trying to seduce me?

***

By the time, I change from the pretty flowered dress I'd worn for dinner and pull a lavender sweatshirt on over black leggings, I've calmed down enough to realize how ridiculous I'm acting. Rhys is simply doing his job, like I should be doing instead of fantasizing like a sixteen-year-old with her first crush. Thank goodness he can't read my mind, or I'd never be able to face him again.

Cool and calm—that's my new mantra.

"*Good luck with that*," my inner pessimist whispers in my ear.

"Hush," I say. "I can change, just watch." And

great, now I'm having conversations with myself. Pathetic, much?

"C'mon, Buttercup. I need you to be my buffer, okay?" I pick up the befuddled pooch and carry her out to the living room.

Rhys is holding her pretty pink rhinestone collar and shaking his head in disgust. "I'm not putting this ugly *thing* on that poor animal. It'll weigh her neck down to the ground for Pete's sake."

Insulted on Buttercup's behalf, I whisk the collar out of his hand and sit on the sofa with the pup on my knees. "It's *not* ugly. You're going to give her a complex."

I push the strap through the buckle and carefully tighten it around the pup's neck. She's a sweetheart and sits still while I complete this maneuver, no thanks to my annoying companion.

"It's too late for that," he says as her ears droop.

I clip the leash Rhys extends to me onto her collar and set her down. She does look kind of pathetic. The collar swamps her skinny neck, poor thing. Oh, well, she'll grow into it.

"Ready?" I ask brightly, rising and moving toward the door. Except... the leash grows taut and stops me in my tracks. I look back to see Buttercup sitting on her haunches and Rhys almost snorting with laughter.

"Not sure she gets the whole going for a walk thing," he guffaws.

My lips twitch, but I manage to withhold my laughter. It's a matter of sisterhood now. "C'mon, Buttercup, show this doubting Thomas how smart you are. I bet there's a bush out there with your name on it."

I give a discreet tug and whether it's the thought of exploring the bushes, or humoring the humans (probably the latter), she stands and trots out the door as though we've done it a thousand times before.

Ha. My raised eyebrow shouts my triumph, but then I have to hurry after her before she pulls the leash out of my fingers.

Rhys chuckles and follows behind. "This should be entertaining."

I'm so happy my discomfort is amusing to him. Just wait until it's his turn to take the reins—or in this case, leash.

We wander down the street in a surprisingly companionable silence, stopping every few feet for Buttercup to investigate the neighborhood scents. I shudder to think what that little black nose is inhaling off the ground, so I turn my attention to my other favorite pastime—snooping in people's windows.

Not everyone is accommodating, but here and there a family has forgotten to pull the curtains and I get a glimpse into their world. A mother urging her kids to bed, a couple sitting at a candlelit table, holding hands and staring into each other's eyes, a man slouched in an old recliner, beer in hand.

"Do you ever wonder what they're thinking?" Rhys asks pensively, following my gaze.

Caught by his tone, I look at his face but it's too dark to see his expression, so I decide to go with honesty. "I used to pretend they were my family. That my mom would be there when I got home from school and Dad would help with my homework. That we'd share meals and laughter and holidays together." I stop and give a sad excuse for a chuckle. "Silly, huh?"

He doesn't laugh with me.

Instead, he does something much worse.

He gently pries Buttercup's leash out of my death grip and slowly tugs me into his arms, wrapping me into his warm embrace, and my heart cracks.

14

Rhys

Georgina is breaking my heart. Although her parents are alive and well, it sounds as though her childhood was as lonely as mine.

Empathy for the stronger-than-she-realizes, beautiful, tempting woman tightens my arms, drawing her close to the staccato beat of my heart. Her body fits against mine as though it's meant to be there—two halves of a whole. I'm not sure what's happening between us, only that I'm not willing to walk away from her, my career be damned.

She shudders and my lips find her brow. "Are you okay?"

She looks up and we freeze, our breath co-mingling. "I am now," she admits softly. "I'm sorry for unloading on you like that."

I grasp her chin, keeping her gaze on mine. "Don't. You have nothing to apologize for. I'm glad you trusted me enough to share what must be painful memories." I gently kiss her mouth, lingering on the pillowy softness of her lips.

A car goes by and honks, breaking us apart. Even though she's only a step away, I miss the warmth of her body next to mine. The ambient streetlight turns the shadows soft and intimate; it could be just the two of us in our own private world.

"Why are you here, Rhys?" Georgina huddles into her sweater and stares as though she's trying to figure me out.

I could tell her not to bother, I'm still working on that myself.

"You invited me, remember?" I crouch down to pet Buttercup, so I don't have to see the frustration on her face.

"Seriously. Shouldn't you be jet-setting around the globe instead of babysitting a new acquisition to your organization?" She placed a hand on my shoulder. "Talk to me. I feel like I've bared my soul to you, but I know virtually nothing about your life. Throw me a bone here, okay?"

She's right. I tend to bottle my emotions inside. After a lifetime of disappointments, I've learned no one cares what I'm going through.

Maybe Georgina is different.

I rise with Buttercup in my arms for support and relay a truth that has haunted me for years. "The night my mother died I was at a college frat party." She bites back a gasp, but I can sense her horror—it lives in my veins.

"Was she ill?" Georgina asks, her eyes reflecting the crescent moon behind my head.

"Cancer. I knew it was coming, we all did. But she died alone. How pathetic is that?" I squeeze the pup too hard and she whimpers. I set her down and watch as she heads off to investigate the shrubbery, no worse for wear. "My dad was at a business meeting downtown, and I was pounding back beer while Mom took her last breath. I've never been able to forgive myself for that." *Or my father*.

She comes closer, offering comfort where none is deserved. I have yet to tell her about the board's plan to dump her business on the open market. When I do, it's going to crush her. It's not going to matter that it wasn't my idea. She'll never want to see me again, and I'm not ready to let her go.

"Your mom wouldn't have wanted you to see her that way. She knew you loved her, Rhys. It's not your fault." She reaches up and cups my bristly jaw, reminding me I need to shave before my video conference meeting with my father tomorrow. "You need to let it go."

Her words, coming so close on the heels of my thoughts turn me inside out. Groaning, I wrap my arms around her and bury my face in the flowery fragrance of her hair. More than anything, I wish we could have met under different circumstances. Ones that didn't include me holding her life's dream on the edge of a ledge with no rappel line.

I have to tell her; I have no choice.

I lean back and gaze into the face that has come to mean so much to me in such a short period of time. If only there was another way.

"So," she says jauntily in an obvious effort to cheer both of us up. "Do you want to hear my brilliant idea for the company?"

I should be getting used to this by now, but still find it disconcerting how much our minds work on the same wavelength.

"Shoot, and I don't mean that literally," I say, holding out no real hope. When she hears CLO's plan, I'll be lucky to get out alive.

"You're silly." She laughs and grabs my hand, tugging me down the street toward a kids' park with a set of swings, a short slide, and climbing equipment.

She takes a seat on the middle swing and gets it to

rock back and forth while I find a good place to tie Buttercup where we can keep an eye on her. Then I stand behind Georgina and give her a couple of pushes, smiling at her simple joy in our surroundings. The women I've dated wouldn't have been caught dead on a child's swing. It's just another way Georgina stands out.

After I get her going with some good height, I hop onto the swing next to hers and try to catch up, feeling carefree—the stress of the last few days fall away.

"So, what's the plan?" I ask, curious to know what she's come up with.

She looks over at me with a smile that stretches practically ear-to-ear. "Sustainability," she says with a flourish, kicking her legs to go higher. "If we can go carbon neutral, we'll be eco-friendly. In today's market, do you realize how important that is?"

Dust swirls around us as she digs her toes into the dirt to slow down. "By dealing with farms that have switched from natural gas and fossil fuel to waste wood to heat their greenhouses, we are effectively lowering our carbon footprint.

"Combine that with organic produce, lean protein, low carb menus and we are showing our responsibility to a healthier population. I'm working on new vegan options, as well as choices for those with dietary restrictions such as wheat or gluten-free, nut allergies, Diabetes. The more we can accommodate these issues with healthy alternatives, the better it will be for our clients—which, in turn, will help to grow our brand." She grins. "Brilliant, right?"

I come to a stop as I digest the information. It's an innovative idea, but she's right. People *are* clamoring for healthier lifestyle choices, and if we market *Bloomin' Right* in that category we could have the next *Fortune 500* on our hands. Depending on our bottom line. CLO will never go for it, if the cost is too high. Still, I can't ruin her excitement right now.

I lean over and grasp her face in my hands. "Better than brilliant, it's bloody genius," I say, then proceed to show her just how extraordinary I think she is.

15

Georgina

Friday morning, I practically skip into work. I'm sure the smile on my face must transmit how besotted I've become with a certain tall, dark, *amazing* entrepreneur and I don't care. Who would have thought I'd meet the man of my dreams trapped in an elevator? Rhys is so much more than I expected. Instead of the cynical businessman, he's shown himself to be kind and caring—and incredibly sexy.

"What's with the smile, boss?" Patty gazes at me quizzically from the receptionist's counter.

"Just happy to be alive," I say, handing over the requisite double, double coffee. "It's Friday, Patty, and I made it up the stairs without tripping. I call that a good start to the day."

Patty grins and takes an appreciative sip of her

brew. "Still don't trust the elevator, huh? If I'd been locked in there with Mr. Turner..." she waves a hand in front of her face, "well, let's just say I could die happy."

"What are you blathering on about now?" Jeremy joins us and bumps shoulders with Patty, nearly overturning her cup.

"Hey, watch it," Patty cries, scrambling to save her precious coffee.

He reaches out to help and accidentally brushes the side of her breast. "Oops," he says, turning about five shades of red. "I, um, guess you, um, have it under control, so I'll just, um, get back to work. Thanks, Georgina," he adds belatedly, grabbing his own takeout cup and beating a hasty departure.

I wait until he's disappeared into the file room to burst into laughter. "Someone has it bad," I note, my gaze on Patty's flushed cheeks and starry eyes.

"Do you think so?" she asks, oblivious. "I keep waiting for him to ask me out, but he never does. It's so frustrating."

"Why don't you ask him out, then?" Tom says before I can offer any advice. "What happened to women's lib?"

He must have arrived while we were in the midst of the coffee debacle. He smells as though he bathed in a forest this morning, and what's with the giant bouquet of sunflowers? Ella's favorite, if I'm not mistaken. Someone is looking for brownie points, for all his tough talk.

"Good morning, Tom," Patty and I chirp at the same time, then look at each other and grin. "You owe me a beer."

"Wow, you're in good humor," he says as though I rarely am—which okay, might be more truthful than I want to admit. "Caught the love bug, have we?"

"You would know," I reply archly, raising my brow at the flowers. "Are those for me?" I say, just to get his goat.

"Quit teasing the poor man," Ella calls, stepping out of her office. "They *better* be for me." She backs the warning with a soft smile and snuggles up to his side for a kiss. "These are beautiful," she murmurs, her dark chocolate eyes alight with adoration.

"I wanted to get you something special, to make up for being a jerk this week," Tom admits. He glances at the peanut gallery (Patty and me), then takes a deep breath before going down on one knee. "Ella, you are the light and soul of my existence. I love you and want to spend the rest of my life proving it—will you marry me?"

We all gasp, including Jeremy, who's returned from the filing room. Tears blur my vision and I wipe at them impatiently, not wanting to miss a moment of this affirmation between my two best friends. If anyone deserves a happily-ever-after, it's them.

"Ella, say something," Tom begs, his heart on his sleeve.

Ella is in shock. Her eyes are huge, the brown orbs reflecting a miniature Tom holding rapidly wilting flowers as he tries not to panic. Her fingers are trembling so bad over her mouth, I'm surprised she's still standing. And then she's not.

Bursting into tears, she drops to her knees and throws herself into Tom's arms. He awkwardly pats her back, the sunflowers suffering in silence, and looks up at us in desperation.

I give him a wet smile and relieve him of the flowers before Ella gets hit with one, then give them both a quick hug and whisper in her ear, "Put the man out of his misery."

"Wha... oh, yes, yes I'll marry you. A thousand times yes," she cries, her face a hot mess.

He takes a handkerchief—gotta love a guy who comes prepared—and a small, blue velvet box out of his pocket and gently wipes her tears before handing it over, his own fingers trembling. "If you don't like it, we can get a different one—"

His voice peters out as she opens the box to discover an exquisite pearl surrounded by diamonds in rose gold.

Ella's mouth drops open. "How did you know?" She stares at him like he's just discovered the secret to the Lost City of Atlantis.

His shoulders sag, the relief palpable. "Your grandmother told me you always loved her wedding set. When she offered it to me, I didn't know what to say. She assured me you would like this better than a new ring, so I took it in and had it cleaned and sized, and then did a lot of praying." He gives a weak chuckle and slowly, carefully slides the engagement ring over her knuckle. "Perfect."

It *is* perfect. It totally suits Ella, and already the pearl seem to like its new home, glowing against her dark skin. I clap as they kiss to seal the deal and hope one day it'll be me saying yes to the man of my dreams. Maybe even Rhys?

We've spent almost every hour of the last three days together, working on our new concept for *Bloomin' Right*, sharing meals, talking, laughing, loving. My pulse sets up a nice little buzz and I look toward the door, half expecting to see him there.

Rhys isn't, but there *is* a stranger in our midst, and he doesn't look happy.

"Hello," I say, adopting my professional face as I step around Tom and Ella, still embraced, turning to see who's here. "May I help you?"

"From what I've seen—" he frowns, "it's no wonder this company is in dire need of a transformation."

"Excuse me?" I sputter, a sick feeling growing in my belly.

"My son told me this is a lost cause. I decided to give you the benefit of the doubt, but now I'm sorry I did."

My knees threaten to crumple. Tom steps forward, his fists bunched, but Ella holds him back. I'm grateful for his support, but we can't afford a lawsuit. Especially against this man if he's who I think he is.

I'm going to have a good crying fit later, but for now I need to ask the question. To know if the thing I fear the most is true.

"Who are you?" I demand, anger and betrayal stiffening my shoulders.

"Rhys didn't tell you?" he asks, knocking me sideways with his words. "I'm his father."

16

Rhys

I go over my notes, for what feels like the hundredth time, in preparation for my father's conference call. Two edicts he's imposed on me over the years; punctuality and preparedness. Funny, I can't remember a time we had a relationship like a *normal* father and son. After hearing all of Georgina's wonderful memories of her grandmother, I feel the loss.

Georgina.

This week has been both a heaven and a hell for me. I'm falling for the one woman guaranteed to hate my guts by the end of our association. Why did I let this happen? I was supposed to come to Seattle, do my job, and get out before the recriminations could rain down on my head.

Instead, I've spent the last few days getting to know the most amazing person I've ever met. Georgina's zest for life is addictive. She took a hands-on approach to showing me the types of food she envisions for her company. We visited the open-air Pike's Place Market to witness a crowd drawer; fishmongers throwing fish before having them wrapped, to customers shocked delight. While there, we also learned about the fish philosophy, created by John Christensen, a business technique to bring happiness to the workplace—something my dad could use. She even managed to get a picture of me wearing a bib over my three-piece suit for a shellfish feast at The Crab Pot.

I feel like a better person around her. She pulls me out of my head, and I get to experience the world through a softer lens. It's... refreshing.

I wanted to do something special to thank her for this week, so I booked a tour of the Space Needle's new feature, The Loupe, with the world's first rotating glass floor. And if we survive that thrill-ride, I've reserved seats for us at a farm-to-table restaurant afterward. I've been doing some research since Georgina shared her ideas and have found some of the top chefs in the country are adopting this method. Logically, cost, convenience, control, and sustainability can all be maintained using this system.

I plan on pitching the idea to my dad at today's

video meeting. If I can get his approval, we could take the program to the next level and use the land adjacent to the warehouse for farming our own environmentally sound, organic crops. We'd need permits, of course, but from a marketing aspect it would be a homerun.

My watch says only half an hour has gone by since the last time I stared at its mocking face. Anxiety gnaws at my gut. This presentation is more important to me than any I've done in the past. I'm hoping—praying, really—that I can change my father's plan to sell *Bloomin' Right* out from under Georgina. But to do that, I have to prove its worth the investment, and I don't know if I can. So, then the question becomes; what am I going to do if I lose the bid?

The phone rings, jarring me from my thoughts. It's Dad's PA. My heart stutters. Dad always calls me direct. Frightening scenarios run through my mind, even as I hurry to answer the call.

"Hello?" I try to keep calm and businesslike but can't control the waver in my voice.

"Mr. Turner, this is Janice from your father's office. I regret to inform you—"

I blanch and look for the nearest place to sit down —the side of my unmade bed. "Is he dead?" I say hoarsely, my eyes blurring.

"What?" she exclaims. "No, your father is very much alive—or he was when he left here this morning."

I shake my head, a hand on my chest. Now I know what my heart would feel like on a defibrillator. "I'm confused. Wasn't I supposed to have a conference call with him today? Where is he?"

Janice gives a gusty sigh. "That's what I've been trying to tell you, Mr. Turner Sr. asked me to inform you of a change of plan. He decided to do a surprise inspection on his new acquisition—*Bloomin' Right*, I believe?" She waits a moment for my reply, but my stomach just dropped to my feet and I stay quiet as I try to grapple with this new development.

"Yes, so he asks that you meet him at the main office promptly at eleven. Do you need the address?" Tap-tapping comes through the line as she no doubt brings up the info on her computer.

I curse under my breath and run a vexed hand through my hair. "No, I don't need the address. What do you think I've been doing for the last week?" I roar to the hapless personal assistant. Count on Dad to make my life miserable.

"Of course, sir," she answers with a haughty air. "Well, if that is all...?"

Other than giving me my last rites, which I'm going to need when Georgina gets through with me? "Next time give a little more notice. Mr. Turner Sr. won't be happy to be kept waiting, and I'll be sure to let him know why I'm late." I hang up with her buts ringing in my ear, and immediately call for an Uber.

Ten-thirty. What are the chances the car will arrive on time, traffic will be light, and I'll beat my dad to Georgina's office?

Not good. Not good at all.

My pulse is a horde of angry hornets beating against the walls of my neck and wrists as I race into the building and jab the elevator button. Why is the damn thing never on the same floor as I am?

A familiar whistling comes from around the corner. The caretaker appears, coffee in hand, and my heart pinches. Georgina's been making deliveries again, I'd wager.

Sam, I think his name is, smiles and glances at the rapidly dropping numbers above the elevator doors. "Going to see my girl, are ya?"

I was hoping she would be *my* girl, at least until today's debacle, but I just go with a nod.

"Well," he says, taking a post with a shoulder against the wall. "There's no one sweeter than Georgina. Last month when my wife was sick, she arranged for meals to be delivered every night. And, she took up a big collection in the building and gifted the proceeds to Beth's care.

"Yep, she deserves to have someone take care of her the way she's always taking care of everyone else." He straightens as the doors ding open. "You keep that in mind now, you hear?"

I stare at him, befuddled, as the doors slide closed and the ascent up ten floors gets under way. How does he know I have a relationship with Georgina? But then I remember how it must have looked when we were rescued by Sam in the locked elevator on Monday, and grin. He's a sly one.

I look at my watch and the smile fades—11:05.

I'm late.

17

Georgina

They look alike: Rhys and his dad. Same widow's peak in their dark hair, though the man in front of me wears his shorter and has distinguished gray streaks. Where Rhys' eyes are a denim blue, his father's are pure steel—cold and analytical.

As an opponent, he would be merciless.

I shiver, then straighten my shoulders. I'm not sure what Rhys has told him, but it's up to me to change Mr. Turner's first impression of our office.

"You're here on a special day, Mr. Turner." I smile, though my jaw aches with the effort. "My assistant managers, Tom and Ella, have just gotten engaged." I turn back to my friends and the smile becomes sincere. "I'm sure you're as thrilled for them as we are."

Mr. Turner clears his throat. "Yes, well, there's a time and a place, but I wish you all the best."

Surprised, I glance at him. That was *almost* nice. Then I remember Rhys mentioning that his mother died when he was young and compassion softens my stance.

"If you'd like to follow me to my office, I can try to correct any misrepresentations you may have heard."

Thanks for nothing, Rhys.

Hurt and anger swarm my chest, making it hard to act normal. How could Rhys pretend to believe in me to my face, and then denigrate me to his father? If I never see him again, it will be too soon. But, at least for now, his father is the CEO and my business partner. He's the one I need to convince.

The trek across the front end never seemed so long. I could feel the weight of Mr. Turner's gaze on my back along with the sympathetic, worried eyes of my staff. They have reason to be concerned; their livelihoods are on the line, as well as our reputation.

I hold the door for my guest, then, with a last longing look back, close us in together. It's not that he scares me—well, okay, maybe a little bit—so much as the pressure I feel to make a good impression because of Rhys—and that annoys the hell out of me.

"Have you been in town long?" I ask, morbidly curious just how long I've been played for a fool.

"This morning," he says, unbuttoning his suit jacket to take a seat across from me the way his son had done earlier this week.

A week.

How could I have been so foolish as to fall in love with a man I obviously didn't know in such a short space of time? Hysterical laughter bubbles up my throat but I choke it back. The elder Mr. Turner already thinks I'm unprofessional, I don't need to add crazy to the list.

"It's a beautiful city. I hope you get the chance to enjoy a few of the attractions before you leave." I don't offer to be the tour guide this time, once was enough. "Let's get down to business, shall we? As I've shown your son, we have a well-run operation consisting of seventeen employees, a warehouse where we package our product, and a growing clientele. While I understand your need to oversee your investment, please remember this is *my* business, Mr. Turner, and, as such, I will make decisions based on what's best for my customers." While it felt good to get that off my chest, I'm now queasy and want nothing more than to put my head between my knees and let the world disappear.

He sits back, crosses his ankle over his knee—another Rhys move, damn him—and applauds my demonstration.

"I can see why my son has been so reticent in our

conversations this week. You have sass, Miss Michaels, I appreciate that."

"It's Ms. but thank you—I think." I'm not sure if sass is a good thing or not.

"Well, *Ms.* Turner, while I appreciate your enthusiasm, the truth of the matter is that your business is floundering. Without our contribution, the overdue payments on your bank loan would have forced you into bankruptcy."

He drops his foot to the floor and leans forward, his smile reminding me of Shark Week on television.

"I'm sure you realize our intervention comes with a price. We lay it out clearly in our contracts—which you signed—that CLO will be the majority shareholder, and, as such, carry final word on all important decisions relative to the business, including the possibility of selling the holdings. You agreed to these terms, I believe?"

"Yes, of course." My fists clench. I know he's aware of my financial history, given the influx of money I received from his corporation, my swirling stomach doesn't welcome Mr. Turner pointing out my deficiencies.

And then the last part of what he said registers.

"Selling?" I mumble, suddenly faint. "Is that a consideration?" My chest hurts and there's a sour taste in my mouth. Maybe I'll have a heart attack and escape the unfolding nightmare.

"My son didn't tell you?" Mr. Turner stares at me, his voice coming from a great distance. "Are you all right, Ms. Michaels?"

Well, at least he got my name right. It'll be necessary for the sales agreement—when he takes my dream and stomps it under his Berluti loafers.

"No, Mr. Turner, I am most definitely *not* all right." I'm on my feet shouting, but I don't care. My life has just imploded. I think I'm allowed a breakdown.

The door bangs open, hitting the wall, and Rhys stands in the opening with Tom and Jeremy close behind.

"What's going on here?" Tom roars, his gaze searching my face.

"Father, what have you done?" Rhys demands, striding into the room. "Georgina, please, let me explain." His expression turns pleading, but I'm too cold to feel its lure.

"Please escort these men from my office, Tom. I believe we're finished here." I turn to Mr. Turner, refusing to meet Rhys' gaze. "I'd prefer any future communication be done through my lawyer, if you don't mind."

He nods and rises to his feet. "Of course. I wish... well, it's been a pleasure." He holds out his hand, and after a hesitation, I accept the handshake. After all, I'm the one wholet my company down, not him.

Tom ushers him out while Jeremy waits uncertainly for Rhys.

"Give us a minute, will you?" Rhys asks and I shrug. There's nothing he can say now. It's too late.

We stare at each other over the expanse of my desk as Jeremy quietly closes the door. Rhys is the first to break the silence.

"So, you've met my dad."

Brilliant deduction, Watson. "Yes, I have," I say, so sweetly sugar wouldn't melt on my tongue. "Imagine my surprise when he informed me my company, the one you and I have worked on all week, is going to be sold." I sink into my chair, the hopelessness of the situation an elephant on my shoulders.

"I know, I'm—"

"So, you did know," I interrupt, my ire rising. "Your father intimated as much, but I thought to myself, no, Rhys wouldn't hide something so literally life-changing from me. He's a standup guy. We're friends, maybe more than friends. That man wouldn't purposely go behind my back with the intention of ruining me, would he?" My fingers are talons, digging holes into the upholstery of my chair when I'd prefer to be ripping his face off right now. Not that I'm normally violent, but...

"Look," he starts again, his neck ruddy. "To be fair, I didn't know you before this week, other than numbers on a spreadsheet. But once we met, I knew you were passionate about this business and, through no fault of your own, suffered because of the market downturn."

He rounds the desk and crouches at my side, his hand closing over mine. I freeze. His proximity, and the warmth of his skin, melts the ice around my heart and lets the pain seep in.

"Give me a chance to fix this, Georgina. You can trust me, I promise."

The words are the ones I want to hear, so why do they sound so empty?

I tug my hand free. "Can you go now? I... don't feel well." Understatement of the year.

He stares at me for an interminable time, then rises to kiss my brow. "I'll call you later?"

Emotion clenches my throat until I can barely breathe. "Sure, later."

The tears I've been holding back trace a path down my face the moment he's out the door.

18

Rhys

My feet drag as I walk through the reception area of *Bloomin' Right*. Georgina's staff stare at me with daggers in their eyes and I can't blame them. I should have been upfront from the start, instead I've hidden behind a mask of deception.

My dad will be so proud.

Ella gets up in my face, her corkscrew curls bouncing with kinetic energy. "How could you betray Georgina like that?"

I back up a step and glance around for reinforcements, but, of course, there are none. "I understand your disappointment, but Georgina—"

"—Is the kindest, gentlest soul on the planet. And you just crushed her heart. I hope you're happy." Ella crosses her arms and lifts her chin. "You owe her an apology, at the very least."

She's right, I do. But first, I need to clarify a few things with my father.

"I have to go," I say, taking a last, pensive look at Georgina's closed door. "Take care of her, will you?"

Ella shakes her head, clearly disgusted with me, but I can't worry about that right now. I need to have a long overdue conversation with Dad and my stomach is churning. I leave the office and the staff's collective wrath behind and hurry toward the bank of elevators.

Tom is striding toward me, but my dad is nowhere in sight.

"Is he gone?" I ask, frustrated because every step takes me further from where I want to be—with Georgina.

Tom is even with me now and, out of nowhere, throws a punch that knocks my head back.

I stumble backward and cup my aching jaw. "What the hell?"

"That's for Georgina," he says, satisfaction ringing in his tone. He shakes out his hand, then tucks it under the other arm. "Damn, that hurts."

I chuckle and taste blood on my tongue. "You split my lip," I say, surprised.

"Here." He hands me a folded napkin from his

pocket. "You going to do something about this mess, or do I need to hit you again?"

I can't help it; I like this guy.

I dab my lip and look despairingly at the elevator. "I'm too late. My father is gone."

Tom shakes his head and nods to a set of doors down the hall I never noticed before. "No, he's not. He wanted to use the restroom before heading to the airport. You have time."

My heart jumps. Am I really going to do this? I've been a toe-the-line son my whole life. The thought of going up against Dad's wishes gives me hives. But I don't have a choice. Georgina deserves the opportunity to succeed, and by damn, I'm going to make sure she gets it.

"Thanks, man," I say, thumping Tom on the back. "Ella's a lucky woman."

He looks at me and the love he feels for his lady is there for God and everyone to see. "Nope. I'm the lucky one. If you do what I think you're going to do, you'll see what I mean."

With that cryptic comment, he walks away, leaving me to face my fears.

I look around and decide the waiting area where Georgina spoke with her friend a few days ago will work as my Alamo.

I'm too nervous to sit, so I stand and stare out the

window at the Seattle skyline. If all goes well (I childishly cross my fingers), I could be calling this city home in the near future. An image of Georgina laughing up at me from the swing in the park on our first pseudo 'date' fills my chest with warmth. We may not have known each other long, but my heart shouts she's the one. I can't walk away without giving our relationship a chance.

"Son?"

My dad's voice jolts me out of my thoughts, and I turn to see him standing in a ray of light streaming through the floor-to-ceiling window. *He looks old.* The man who's always been bigger than life to me suddenly seems somehow... diminished. The resentment that has festered inside of me for so long fades, leaving compassion in its wake. We may not see eye-to-eye on his business practices, but he's always been there for me. I just hope that holds true today.

"Dad, we need to talk."

He moves his cuff to glance at his watch and frowns. "Can't it wait? I have a flight—"

"No," I say, interrupting. "It needs to be now. I don't plan on leaving Seattle any time soon."

"Well," he murmurs, "what brought this on—or need I ask?" His head tips toward the *Bloomin' Right* doors and I flush. "She's a beautiful woman."

"It's not like that," I snap, then sigh. "I care about

her, Dad. She's... important to me." I'm not about to confess my love for Georgina to him when I've barely acknowledged it myself. "Sit with me, please?"

Another hesitation, then he shrugs and takes a chair—no cozy sofas for *my* dad. "Fine but make it quick. You know how I hate to be late."

I smile, for once not bothered by his stern demeanor. "The sky won't fall if you run a few minutes behind time, you know."

He looks at me startled. "I realize that, son. But my father was a stickler for the rules, and I guess I've let it carry over into my life."

And mine. But at least now I know the reason behind the attitude. I stare at the entrance to *Bloomin' Right*, at a loss for how to start this critical conversation. There's so much riding on the outcome. What if I...?

"Just spit it out, boy. What is it you have to tell me that couldn't wait until later?" Impatience practically drips from his pores, but instead of freezing me in my tracks it has the opposite effect and the gears in my head start turning.

"Dad, I want to buy you out." His shocked expression gives me a spurt of adrenaline. "Not CLO, I only want the shares to *Bloomin' Right*. I'll pay you fair and square, but then that's it, I'm leaving the corporation."

There, I've said it. I'm so giddy, a bottle of champagne would have nothing on the bubbles exploding in my chest. The ball and chain of corporate life is broken, and I feel like I can soar above the clouds in the sky. I should feel guilty, but I know my father can easily replace my position. I am far from indispensable, and I thank my lucky stars for that reality.

"But… what about everything we've worked toward?" Dad shakes his head, trying to take it all in. "When will I see you?"

My heart expands at those words. I reach across and clasp his knee. "Any time you want, Dad. I'm still your son. You just won't be able to bully me around anymore." I grin to show I'm teasing.

"She means this much to you, then?" He looks at me with the memory of my mom swimming in his eyes and I have to go with the truth.

"She means everything."

19

Georgina

I don't know how long I stare blankly at the wall across from me, but a quiet knock on the door has me scrambling to wipe the tears from my cheeks.

"Come in," I call when I feel a semblance of control.

Ella pokes her head in and gives me a tentative smile. "Want to go for a drink?"

I shake my aching head. Crying always makes me feel like I've been run over by a truck. "Rain-check? I think I'll head home and check on Buttercup."

She slips into the room and closes the door. "Honey, do you think you're being fair to him? Rhys seems genuinely sorry for what happened. I think if you give him a chance to explain..."

"Not you, too." I stand and gather my purse and keys. "I thought you were on my side."

Ella moves so I can open the door. "I *am* on your side, which is how I know if you don't talk to him, you'll regret it for the rest of your life."

"I can't, at least not today." I give her a hug, breathing in the familiar jasmine-scented shampoo she swears keeps her curls under control. "Love you, E."

She tightens her hold around me, before letting go. "I'll call you tomorrow. Pick up your phone."

I chuckle. "Yes, ma'am. See you later."

I manage the gauntlet of commiserating gazes with a faint smile meant to look reassuring, and escape into the hall with a sigh of relief.

A short-lived sigh.

Rhys is near the waiting area, his back to me. My skin comes alive, tingling to be in his arms again. I need to get out of here; now.

I edge along the wall to the elevators and press the down button. *Hurry. Hurry.* I would have taken the stairs if they weren't so close to the lounge.

Ding. The bell announces our floor and the elevator door slides open.

"Georgina, wait."

Rhys voice is dismayingly close. I jab the button, hoping against hope to lock him out. Of course, it's not to be. His fingers grasp the door and it slides, allowing him entry. Frustrated, I press for the main floor and meld my back to the wall, as far away from him as I can get.

The silence is oppressive. I'm dying here. Ten floors could be a hundred for how long this is taking. Then the elevator jerks to a stop and my stomach drops through the floor.

"What hap—" My eyes bulge. Rhys' hand is over the emergency stop button and I realize he's the cause of our current predicament. "What are you doing?" I screech, more upset about being stuck with him than hanging in the middle of an elevator shaft.

"We aren't going anywhere until you hear me out," he says, his expression fierce as he grips the rail.

"Where's your sidekick?" I snarl, my calm façade gone.

"My father left for the airport. He wants to get home before it grows late. He hates driving after dark."

I stare at him, sensing a shift in his ambivalence with his father. I hope for Rhys' sake they have resolved some of their differences. I know their estrangement bothers him. We may be over, but I don't wish him ill. Well, maybe a random flu bug...

"Hello in elevator two. What is the emergency, please?" Sam's voice disturbs our staring contest and I grasp at the interruption.

"Hey, Sam. It's Georgina." I glance at the emergency button. "I, umm, bumped the red button, I'm sorry."

"Oh, dear. Well give me a minute to reset the lever and we'll get you down. Call if you need anything at all." After that rather odd statement, Sam hangs up and I'm left in a too-small elevator with the man I'm trying to hate.

"Look, I made some mistakes, and I get that you're angry, but..."

I glower. "But it was all done in the name of business—is that what you were going to say? Because I call bull-crap on that. You *know* I have a good business plan. All I need is the chance to get it off the ground. Did you tell that to your father, Rhys? Did you explain how we worked together to come up with a concept that consumers will buy? Did you defend me at all?"

He takes the two steps that brings him into my space, and gently tips my chin up so he can see my eyes. "I didn't have to defend you," he says. "My father knows how I feel."

He reaches into the pocket inside his jacket and withdraws a set of papers. "This is preliminary, the final paper will arrive next week, but I wanted you to have these today."

He hands them to me, and I stare at him, confused. "What is this?"

His smile is soft. "Open it and you'll see."

I unfold the documents with trembling fingers and try to take in what they seem to be telling me. "These are a bill of sale. They say I own *Bloomin' Right*, loan paid in full. How is this possible?" My eyes are blurring again and I blame it on my glasses. It can't be the tears wetting my cheeks. "What did you do?"

He uses his thumbs to brush the moisture away before giving me a butterfly kiss on the lips. Then he lets me go and steps back to the opposite side of the car and grips the rails. I remember he's scared of enclosed spaces, which makes the fact he pulled that emergency button even more significant. If I can just take a moment to make sense of it all.

"The business is yours. Father decided it was better off in your capable hands than sold to the highest bidder. You can follow your dream now, Georgina. No one will stop you."

I look down at the papers again, but that's all they are—papers. The dream I chased for so many years isn't the wish of my heart.

That dream is in front of me and I stretch out my arms to grab it before it disappears.

I let the bill of sale fall to the floor and rush into Rhys' waiting arms. "Were you really going to let me go?"

"Not on your life," he says, before sweeping me up

in a kiss that curls my toes. "I've left CLO. Do you have any openings for a brilliant financial planner?"

I tip my head and smile. "Why, do you know one?" My heart is so full, I think I could float if Rhys didn't hold on.

"I might," he murmurs against my mouth. "Does the job come with perks?"

"It could," I whisper. "For the right candidate."

He proceeds to show just how perfect he is for the position and we're still wrapped in each other's arms when the elevator opens on the tenth floor to a round of cheers from all our friends.

I guess dreams and wishes do come true.

AFTERWORD

Reviews are the lifeblood of any successful author. Without you, we can't be heard.

If you enjoy the story, please consider sharing on your favorite social media sites, as well as GoodReads and from wherever you've bought the book.

Thank you,

Jacquie Biggar

Jacqbiggar.com

PREVIEW SKATING ON THIN ICE

Mac Wanowski was having the best night of his hockey career. Two goals and three assists with a period and a half to go. Everything was going their way. He should be a shoo-in for MVP. The Victoria WarHawks were playing on home turf to a full stadium of rowdy fans with fast ice—nothing could stop him now.

The blow came out of nowhere.

One minute he was flying down the ice with the puck held in the sweet spot of his stick, the crowd roaring his name, the net in sight, in the next instant Mac was shoved from behind and smacked into the boards. He bounced and went down hard on his right knee. The pain was immediate and intense. It sucked the breath from his lungs and left him seeing stars. He dropped his head between his arms and tried to remain conscious until the medics arrived. It was small consolation the refs caught the illegal move and rang the penalty buzzer.

Fricking Murtagh.

The other team's enforcer liked to pull sneak attacks. He'd done it before. Mac rolled onto his back and blinked as the auditorium swam before his eyes.

"Wow, man, that had to hurt." Samson chortled, skidding to a stop against the boards. The plexi-glass shook with the collision.

Edwards, the team's doctor skated across the ice in his dress shoes and dropped to his side. "Hey, Hammer, nice hit. How you doing?"

"Been better," Mac grumbled. He squinted through the face-shield and yanked off his gloves. "It's the knee, Doc. Screwed it good this time." The helmet came next, clattering onto the ice along with his dreams.

"Don't worry. He will pay." Lazlo, the grinder, towered over Mac glaring at the other team as though daring them to come near.

"Keep it clean, boys," the ref said, gliding up to pat the Croatian's arm. "I don't wanna send you to the bench, but I will." He exchanged a look with the doc, then blew his whistle and waved an arm over his head. "Gurney's on the way."

Mac growled and tried to sit up, but Edwards forced him down. The guy might be old but working around a bunch of hockey players kept him in shape. "Take it easy, Mac. It's just a precaution. You don't want to aggravate that tendon any more than you need to."

Getting hauled off the ice like an invalid only added insult to injury. Not even the crowd's support could ease his wrath against the meathead who'd taken him down. He strained to see past the EMT's hold on the gurney. Murtagh sat in the penalty box, his arrogant gaze triumphant even as his coach tore him a new asshole from over his shoulder.

Pissed, Mac pointed and mouthed, "You're mine." Then they were in the hallway heading toward the dressing room and his adrenaline waned, leaving him drawn and listless. The knee throbbed, pressing uncomfortably against his protective padding. His shoulder ached from smashing into the wall and his insides jiggled like a bowl full of jelly. But if Doc gave him the go-ahead he could still make the third period. He needed to get out there and support his team, dammit.

Coach was waiting when he arrived, pacing and muttering while running a hand over his thinning pate. The second the EMTs set him down on the exam table Coach was breathing in his face.

"What the hell, Wanowski? I told you to pass! This superhero complex of yours is costing the team. Now what are we supposed to do, huh? We're already two men down and play-offs are coming up. Your actions tonight might have cost us the season. How do you feel now, asshole?"

Like shit, thanks for asking. The man had it in for him ever since Mac hooked up with his daughter for one never-to-be-repeated night, and nothing he did for the team was enough. It bothered him that this time Coach was right—he'd screwed up. Not that he could admit it, especially with all the interested ears wagging in the room. So, he said nothing.

The coach threw up his hands and stormed out of the room, heading back to what was left of the game.

Mac just hoped they could retain their five-three lead until it ended.

"You like playing with fire, don't ya?" Doc Edwards shook his head. "Your contract is almost up with the WarHawks, Mac. Have you given any thought to what comes next?"

Mac frowned at the doc's back as he turned away to open his medical bag. "You hear something you want to tell me about?" He'd given three of his best years to this team. If the franchise planned to trade him off, the least they could do was tell him to his face.

Doc held up his hand. "Don't get your shorts in a knot, kid. I merely meant you can't play hockey forever. You must have a backup plan, right?'

Kid. Mac grunted as the other man loosened the ties on his knee guard. The resulting relief was quickly replaced by agony as blood rushed to the injury. He clenched his fists against the cool metal of the exam table and stared at the ceiling with its ugly track lighting while Doc poked and prodded the area like a sadist.

No, he didn't have a backup plan—this was it for him. Hockey was in his blood. It fed his dark soul and gave him the only true joy he'd ever known.

He couldn't leave the game.

"How bad, Doc?" He tipped his head to look down the length of his body and swore. Just as he'd thought, the knee was swollen and already showing signs of bruising. Last time he'd injured it, he'd ended up with water under the kneecap and had to have it drained. Fun times.

Edwards snapped an ice pack into action and set it against his skin before meeting his worried gaze. "I won't know for sure until we do x-rays. My best guess is your ACL." Mac winced. "Hopefully it's a sprain instead of a full tear which would mean surgery and months of rehab."

Christ, just what he didn't need right now. He laid down and covered his eyes with his forearm. "And if it's a sprain?"

"Sorry, Mac. You're still looking at two-to-four weeks recovery time, physio, and preferably crutches. I know someone, Sam Walters, who's good at this sort of injury. I'll call and see what I can get lined up."

Mac let him drone on with his voice of doom, meanwhile inside his stomach twisted into their own disastrous knots.

What was he going to do now?

Pick up your copy today!

FREE DOWNLOAD

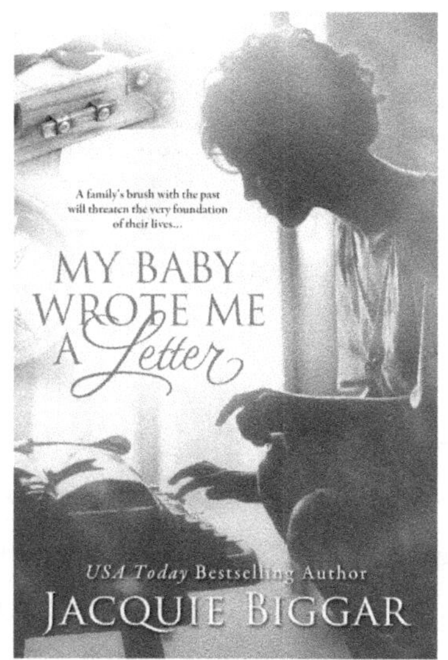

My Baby Wrote Me A Letter

A family's brush with the past will threaten the fabric of their lives.

Eight months pregnant and her Navy husband away on a mission, Grace Freeman craves the security of her childhood home in Canada.

When a letter written by her long-lost mother is found in an old writing desk it creates a tear in the fabric of her family.

Can Grace find a way to bring peace to those she loves, or will a message from the past destroy their future?

Newsletter subscribers also get bonus content and insider information every month. I love giveaways and there is lots of interesting stuff for me to share with you!

Newsletter- Sign up Now!

ABOUT THE AUTHOR

JACQUIE BIGGAR is a USA Today bestselling author of Romantic Suspense who loves to write about tough, alpha males and strong, contemporary women willing to show their men that true power comes from love.

She is the author of the popular Wounded Hearts series and has just started a new series in paranormal suspense, Mended Souls.

She has been blessed with a long, happy marriage and enjoys writing romance novels that end with happily-ever-afters.

Jacquie lives in paradise along the west coast of

Canada with her family and loves reading, writing, and flower gardening. She swears she can't function without coffee, preferably at the beach with her sweetheart. :)

Sign up now to keep up with Jacquie's new releases, excerpts, giveaways, and more:

Newsletter

jacqbiggar.com
jbiggar@jacqbiggar.com

ALSO BY JACQUIE BIGGAR

Wounded Hearts Series

Tidal Falls

The Rebel's Redemption

Twilight's Encore

The Sheriff Meets His Match

Summer Lovin'

Wounded Hearts Box Set

Maggie's Revenge

With This Heart

Mended Souls Series

The Guardian

The Beast Within

Virtually Gone

Gambling Hearts

Hold 'Em

Crazy Little Thing Called Love

My Girl

Married to The Texan- Box set

Blue Haven

Sweetheart Cove

Sunset Beach

Men of WarHawks

Skating on Thin Ice

The Player

Single Titles

Silver Bells

The Lady Said No

My Baby Wrote Me A Letter

Tempted by Mr. Wrong

Valentine: A Hearts and Kisses Romance

Mistletoe Inn

The Sister Pact

Perfectly Imperfect

www.ingramcontent.com/pod-product-compliance
Lightning Source LLC
Chambersburg PA
CBHW072240190626
46809CB00018B/2854

9781988126449